FOR ACTION AND ADVENTURE

DIVE! DIVE! DIVE!

**Commando**

FOR ACTION AND ADVENTURE

# DIVE! DIVE! DIVE!

## THREE OF THE BEST SUBMARINE COMMANDO COMIC BOOK ADVENTURES

**EDITED** BY CALUM LAIRD, EDITOR OF COMMANDO

**CARLTON**
BOOKS

Published in 2012 by Carlton Books Limited
An imprint of the Carlton Publishing Group
20 Mortimer Street
London
W1T 3JW

A catalogue record for this book is available from the British Library.

ISBN: 978 1 84732 969 1

Printed and bound by CPI Group (UK) Ltd, Croydon, CR0 4YY

# Contents

# Introduction

You have to admire men who go to war in submarines. Trusting their lives to a thin cylinder of steel under countless fathoms of water takes an extraordinary level of courage. And that's before the enemy starts lobbing depth charges at them. That's probably why submarine stories make such good material for Commando. The characters in them have already proved themselves by signing up for undersea service and yet they go above (or should that be below) and beyond every time.

The only problem for a comic book, though, is that the action could easily end up as a series of repetitive frames showing endless views of submarine control rooms or men in conning towers searching the horizon. That reckons without the skill of Commando's authors. Thanks to their efforts, the submariners get into scrapes on the land as well as at sea – as you can read in these three classic tales.

"Java Sea Jinx" adds a bit of magic and mystery to the shooting action you'd expect from Commando. Throw in a sailor who poisons his crewmates against their new commander, a Commando raid gone wrong that the Navy has to put right, a rescue and… oh, go on, read it for yourself, there's too much going on to get it all in here!

British submarine *Trent* – operating in the Mediterranean – looks like she might

RUTHLESSLY PATIENT, MORRISON USED HIS SUPERIOR SPEED TO CLOSE THE RANGE — THEN HE FIRED...

...AND TWO WELL-PLACED TORPEDOES SMASHED INTO THE HULL OF THE JAP SUB.

have an easier time of it in "The Silent Service". Lieutenant-Commander Tony Newman seems to have a straightforward mission to land a party of raiders on the shores of North Africa, stay hidden and return to pick them up. Dangerous, yes, but not out of the ordinary for a submarine crew. However, this is Commando so there's a twist when everything goes wrong and the reader is treated to a sea chase and a treasure hunt under hostile guns.

Back in the Far East, "Dive! Dive! Dive!" has a helping of almost everything the other two have. There's also the suspicion that HMS *Tamarin* may have sunk a US sub to add some spice – as if there wasn't enough already. For the icing on the cake, salt-water crocodiles that aren't fussy what (or who) they eat add a dimension of danger beyond depth charges, chlorine gas and fighting-mad Japanese.

So, clear your conning tower, secure your hatches and flood your tanks… in other words, "Dive! Dive! Dive!" as Commando goes underwater.

*Calum Laird*

Calum G Laird
Commando Editor

# WARSHIPS OF WORLD WAR 2

## No. 51: Motor Torpedo Boat (Britain)

Displacement 49 tons.
Length 22.25m (73 feet).
Speed 40 knots.
Crew 13.

Armament — 1 57mm (6-pdr):
twin 20mm (.79-inch):
2 twin 7.6mm (.303-inch):
2 torpedoes in tubes.

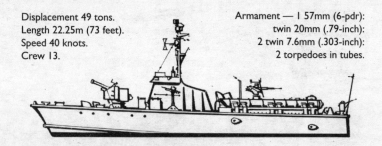

## No. 52: Patrol Toredo Boat (U.S.A.)

Armament — 1 40mm (1.57-inch):
1 20mm (.79-inch):
2 twin 12.7mm (.5-inch):
2 mortars for smoke or H.E.:
4 torpedoes (in launching racks,
not tubes.)

Displacement 45 tons.
Length 24.4m (80 feet).
Speed 40 knots.
Crew 14.

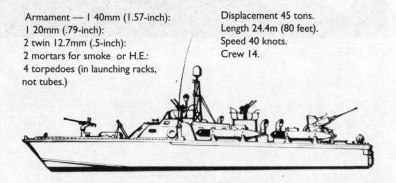

LIEUTENANT BRAD COOPER OF THE AMERICAN NAVY WAS THE SYREN'S PASSENGER ON THIS VOYAGE. HE WAS TO BE LANDED ALONE AND IN SECRET ON THE ENEMY-HELD LIBYAN COAST TO UNDERTAKE A VITAL MISSION.

BUT THERE WAS TROUBLE IN STORE, FOR THE BRITISH SUB HAD BEEN SEEN BY THE WATCHFUL EYES OF THE LOOKOUTS ON A PATROLLING GERMAN E-BOAT, AND THE ENEMY COMMANDER WAS COMING IN TO ATTACK AT TOP SPEED.

THE SUBMARINE'S LOOKOUT SUDDENLY SAW THE DEADLY E-BOAT IN THE MOONLIGHT, AND THE TRACK OF THE TORPEDOES HEADING TOWARDS THE SYREN.

TWO TORPEDOES, HEADING STRAIGHT FOR US.

GET BELOW, LIEUTENANT. MOVE!

IT'S GOING TO BE A CLOSE THING, CAPTAIN!

EVEN AS THE ALARM SOUNDED, THE SUB'S CREW WERE PREPARING TO CRASH DIVE.

BUT THEY WEREN'T QUICK ENOUGH. BEFORE ANYONE COULD GET BELOW, ONE OF THE TORPEDOES STRUCK, RIPPING OPEN THE SYREN'S HULL.

WE'RE GOING TO GO DOWN LIKE A STONE. OVER THE SIDE, LIEUTENANT. IT'S YOUR ONLY CHANCE!

WHAT ABOUT THE REST OF YOU?

THE SYREN'S COMMANDER WAS CONCERNED ONLY WITH THE SURVIVAL OF HIS AMERICAN PASSENGER. IN A FEW SECONDS THE SUBMARINE WOULD BE ON HER WAY TO THE BOTTOM FOR THE VERY LAST TIME, AND IT WAS DOUBTFUL IF ANY OF HER CREW WOULD SURVIVE THE DISASTER.

DON'T ARGUE, MAN. OVER YOU GO!

NO— ARGHH!

COOPER HIT THE WATER HEAVILY, BUT SOON RECOVERED HIS WITS AND SWAM HURRIEDLY AWAY TO AVOID BEING DRAGGED DOWN WHEN THE SUB SANK.

WITHIN SECONDS THE SUBMARINE SLID BENEATH THE WAVES, AND COOPER WAS ALONE IN THE WARM WATER. THE E-BOAT THROTTLED BACK, AND CIRCLED THE AREA WARILY.

SHE'S GONE, HERR KAPITAN. SHE SANK LIKE A STONE.

OVER THERE. I CAN SEE SOMEONE IN THE WATER!

THEY'VE SEEN ME!

THE E-BOAT HALTED NEAR COOPER WHO SWAM GRATEFULLY TOWARDS IT.

CATCH HOLD OF THE HOOK!

I'VE GOT IT!

THE GERMANS WERE SYMPATHETIC. THEY WERE ALL SEAMEN, AND COULD VERY WELL FIND THEMSELVES IN THE SAME SITUATION AT ANY TIME.

HERE, DRINK THIS.

BRING HIM DOWN TO THE WARD ROOM. I WANT TO ASK HIM SOME QUESTIONS!

THE E-BOAT COMMANDER QUESTIONED COOPER, HOPING TO GET SOME INFORMATION ABOUT THE SUNKEN SUB. BUT HE WAS ASTONISHED AT WHAT HE HEARD.

I AM LIEUTENANT BRAD COOPER, UNITED STATES NAVY. THAT IS ALL THE INFORMATION I HAVE TO GIVE YOU, CAPTAIN.

UNITED STATES NAVY? BUT OF COURSE, I SEE THAT BY YOUR UNIFORM. I DID NOT KNOW THERE WERE AMERICAN SUBMARINES IN THE MEDITERRANEAN!

THE E-BOAT CAPTAIN WAS PLEASED, FOR ALTHOUGH COOPER WOULD GIVE HIM NO INFORMATION, HE FIRMLY BELIEVED HE HAD SUNK THE FIRST AMERICAN SUBMARINE TO ENTER IN THESE WATERS.

THAT IS GOOD ENOUGH FOR ME. I AM ONLY CONCERNED WITH THE VICTORY. YOU WILL BE LANDED AND INTERROGATED BY PEOPLE BETTER QUALIFIED FOR THE JOB THAN I.

SO COOPER WAS PUT UNDER GUARD AND THE E-BOAT TURNED AND MADE FOR THE NEAREST PORT.

IT WASN'T LONG BEFORE BRITISH INTELLIGENCE PIECED TOGETHER WHAT HAD HAPPENED, AND THE NEXT DAY IN ALEXANDRIA, WHERE H.M. SUBMARINE " TRENT " LAY AT ANCHOR—

IS THIS H.M. SUBMARINE TRENT, COMMANDING OFFICER, LIEUTENANT-COMMANDER NEWMAN?

YES, SIR. THE CAPTAIN'S IN HIS CABIN.

THE YOUNG OFFICER SOON FOUND LIEUTENANT-COMMANDER TONY NEWMAN, WHO WAS IN HIS CABIN.

I'M NEWMAN. WHAT CAN I DO FOR YOU?

I AM HERE TO TAKE YOU TO FLOTILLA H.Q., SIR. I HAVE NO FURTHER INFORMATION. IT ALL SEEMS RATHER HUSH-HUSH.

DONNING A CLEAN UNIFORM, TONY WAS DRIVEN TO THE HEADQUARTERS OF THE FLOTILLA WHERE A COMMODORE WAS WAITING TO SEE HIM.

AH, COME IN, NEWMAN. THIS IS CAPTAIN CONNORS OF THE COMMANDOS.

WHAT IS IT? SOME KIND OF SECRET MISSION FOR US?

TONY HAD INTENDED THE QUESTION AS A JOKE BECAUSE OF THE PRESENCE OF THE COMMANDO CAPTAIN. BUT IT WAS TO BE A SECRET MISSION FOR H.M. SUBMARINE TRENT WITH VERY LITTLE HUMOUR IN THE DAYS TO COME.

YOU WILL SAIL TO THE ENEMY-HELD PORT OF HABBIBAH IN LIBYA, AND FROM THEN ON YOU WILL ACT UNDER THE ORDERS OF CAPTAIN CONNORS . . .

. . . UNTIL ME AND MY COMMANDOS BRING ON BOARD AN AMERICAN NAVY LIEUTENANT FROM THE TOWN PRISON.

THOSE WERE THE ONLY ORDERS TONY WAS GIVEN AND HE HURRIED BACK TO THE DOCKYARD TO HAVE THE SUB MADE READY FOR SEA. AS HE STOOD ON THE BRIDGE, HIS SECOND-IN-COMMAND, LIEUTENANT TERRY WHITE, SPOTTED AN ARMY TRUCK DRAWING UP ON THE QUAYSIDE.

IT LOOKS LIKE OUR COMMANDOS HAVE ARRIVED.

WE WON'T STAND ON CEREMONY, TERRY. I'LL GET THEM ABOARD AND YOU CAN SETTLE THEM IN THEIR QUARTERS.

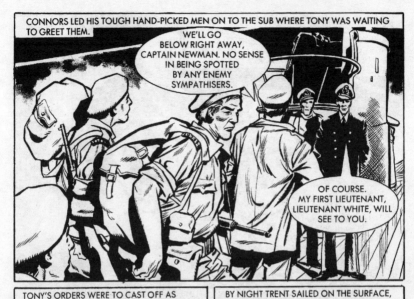

CONNORS LED HIS TOUGH HAND-PICKED MEN ON TO THE SUB WHERE TONY WAS WAITING TO GREET THEM.

WE'LL GO BELOW RIGHT AWAY, CAPTAIN NEWMAN. NO SENSE IN BEING SPOTTED BY ANY ENEMY SYMPATHISERS.

OF COURSE. MY FIRST LIEUTENANT, LIEUTENANT WHITE, WILL SEE TO YOU.

TONY'S ORDERS WERE TO CAST OFF AS SOON AS HIS COMMANDO PASSENGERS WERE ON BOARD AND HE WAS SOON UNDER WAY, WATCHED BY THE VERY ANXIOUS COMMODORE.

IF THIS DOESN'T WORK THE U.S. GOVERNMENT STAND TO LOSE FIVE MILLION DOLLARS!

BY NIGHT TRENT SAILED ON THE SURFACE, KEEPING A SHARP LOOKOUT FOR ENEMY PLANES OR PATROL BOATS. ON THE BRIDGE TONY QUIZZED CONNORS.

IS THERE ANYTHING ELSE YOU CAN TELL ME ABOUT THIS MISSION?

THE AMERICAN IS VERY IMPORTANT, NEWMAN, AND WE'VE GOT TO BRING HIM BACK SAFE.

CONNORS WENT ON TO EXPLAIN THAT HE AND HIS COMMANDOS INTENDED TO LAND ON THE BEACH CLOSE TO HABBIBAH, AT THE SAME TIME AS A LARGE COMMANDO FORCE LANDED TO THE EAST TO CAUSE A DIVERSION BY RAIDING A GERMAN FUEL DEPOT.

THIS WILL TAKE THE GERMANS AWAY FROM HABBIBAH, GIVING ME A CHANCE TO GET INTO THE PRISON, GET THE AMERICAN OUT, AND GET BACK TO YOUR SUB.

WHY COULDN'T THE COMMANDO FORCE HAVE RAIDED HABBIBAH ITSELF?

THE COMMANDO CAPTAIN EXPLAINED THAT A FULL SCALE ATTACK ON HABBIBAH ITSELF WOULD HAVE BEEN TOO INVOLVED, WITH THE CHANCE THAT THE AMERICAN OFFICER MIGHT BE KILLED IN THE FIGHTING.

. . . SO THIS WAY IS EASIER. THE ITALIAN OFFICER COMMANDING THE PRISON GUARD HAS BEEN BRIBED BY BRITISH INTELLIGENCE, AND WILL HAND COOPER OVER WHEN WE COME FOR HIM.

THE WAY YOU TELL IT, IT SOUNDS SIMPLE.

AND CONNORS FERVENTLY HOPED IT WOULD BE JUST THAT.

TWO DAYS LATER THEY WERE OFF THE PORT OF HABBIBAH. BUT THEY HAD TO GO IN CLOSE, AND THERE LAY A DANGER, AS TONY POINTED OUT.

THE WHOLE OF THIS AREA IS MINED, EXCEPT FOR ONE NARROW CHANNEL—AND WE DON'T KNOW ITS LOCATION. SO WE HAVE TO GO IN SLOW AND DEEP.

UNDER THE MINE-FIELD? WELL, I SUPPOSE IT'S SAFER THAN TRYING TO GO THROUGH IT.

THE JOURNEY UNDER THE MINE-FIELD WAS FRAUGHT WITH DANGER. ONE TOUCH ON THE HORN OF A MINE WOULD SET THE THING OFF, AND THE RESULTING EXPLOSION WOULD BLOW THE SUBMARINE APART.

EASY NOW. IF WE HIT A CABLE WE COULD PULL A MINE DOWN ON TOP OF US.

THEN A SUDDEN GRATING ALONG THE SUB'S METAL HULL CAUSED EVERYONE TO HOLD THEIR BREATH

WHAT THE DEVIL'S THAT NOISE, NEWMAN?

A MINE CABLE. IT'S MOVING ALONG OUR HULL. SLOW AHEAD—WE DON'T WANT TO PULL THE MINE DOWN!

A MINE CABLE HAD SNAGGED AROUND THE PERISCOPE, AND AT THAT MOMENT THE SUBMARINE'S CREW AND PASSENGERS NEVER KNEW HOW CLOSE TO DEATH THEY WERE.

EASY NOW . . .

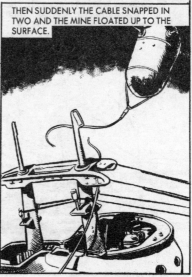

THEN SUDDENLY THE CABLE SNAPPED IN TWO AND THE MINE FLOATED UP TO THE SURFACE.

WHEN THEY HEARD NO MORE SCRAPING, ALL ON BOARD THE SUB BREATHED A SIGH OF RELIEF. TONY WAS SURE THE DANGER WAS NOW OVER.

I THINK WE'RE THROUGH IT NOW. UP PERISCOPE. I WANT TO TAKE A LOOK AT THE COAST.

THERE'S NOT MUCH TIME TO WASTE, NEWMAN. THE COMMANDOS WILL BE GOING ASHORE AT THE FUEL DEPOT SOON.

SO THE SUB BEGAN TO SURFACE, SAFELY INSIDE THE MINEFIELD. BUT HER CAPTAIN WAS UNAWARE OF THE SEVERED MINE, DRIFTING SLOWLY INSHORE ON THE SLOW CURRENT.

THE MINE FLOATED OUT OF SIGHT TOWARDS THE SHORE AS TONY REACHED THE BRIDGE.

HE WAS FOLLOWED BY CONNORS AND TERRY, AND FROM FURTHER ALONG THE COAST THEY COULD HEAR THE SOUNDS OF GUNFIRE, AND SEE FIRES WHICH BLAZED IN THE SKY.

THE RAID IS RIGHT ON TIME, CONNORS. THE HABBIBAH GARRISON OUGHT TO BE ON THEIR WAY TO THE FUEL DEPOT BY NOW.

SOONER WE GET ASHORE THE BETTER. WE'LL BE BACK AS SOON AS WE'VE GOT THE AMERICAN OUT OF PRISON.

ON DECK THE COMMANDOS LAUNCHED THEIR RUBBER DINGHY INTO THE SEA, AND CAPTAIN CONNORS GAVE TONY A FINAL WAVE.

THIS SHOULDN'T TAKE MORE THAN AN HOUR. WE'LL SIGNAL YOU ON OUR WAY BACK TO THE SUB.

I'LL BE WATCHING OUT FOR YOU. GOOD HUNTING!

BUT NOW, THOUGH THEY DID NOT KNOW IT, BETWEEN SUBMARINE AND SHORE-LINE WAS THE DARK, OMINOUS BULK OF THE HORNED MINE.

AFTER PADDLING THEIR DINGHY AROUND FOR TEN MINUTES, TONY SAW A BODY FLOATING IN THE WATER.

SOMETHING OVER THERE—PADDLE TOWARDS IT!

SEE IT, SIR.

THE SURVIVOR WAS CONNORS WHO WAS BADLY INJURED.

DARNED MINE, LOOSE . . .

TAKE IT EASY, CONNORS. WE'VE GOT YOU NOW. WE'LL SEE IF WE CAN FIND ANYBODY ELSE BEFORE WE GO BACK.

BUT THEY FOUND NO OTHER SURVIVORS OF THE DISASTER. CONNORS WAS THE ONLY ONE OF THE RAIDERS ALIVE, AS TONY TOLD HIS SECOND-IN-COMMAND WHEN HE RETURNED TO THE SUB.

IT'S CONNORS, TERRY. THEY HIT A FLOATING MINE. THE REST MUST HAVE BEEN KILLED INSTANTLY.

NO MORE TO DO BUT GO BACK TO ALEX, TONY. THIS IS ONE MISSION THAT'S FAILED.

IN SPITE OF HIS INJURIES, CAPTAIN CONNORS DID NOT WANT
TO BE TAKEN BACK TO ALEXANDRIA AND HOSPITAL. HE HAD
COME TO HABBIBAH TO DO A JOB, AND WAS DETERMINED
THAT IT WOULD BE DONE.

BUT WE'VE GOT TO RETURN, CONNORS. YOU NEED EXPERT TREATMENT AS SOON AS POSSIBLE.

NO— LISTEN NEWMAN. WE MUST FREE THAT AMERICAN OFFICER TONIGHT. THERE WON'T BE ANOTHER CHANCE.

THE COMMANDO WAS INSISTENT. HABBIBAH MUST BE ALMOST DESERTED NOW AND MAJOR
BORTI, THE ITALIAN OFFICER WHO HAD BEEN BRIBED TO RELEASE HIS PRISONER, MUST BE
WAITING ANXIOUSLY, DREADING THE RETURN OF HIS GERMAN ALLIES.

THERE'S ONLY ONE WAY, NEWMAN. YOU MUST DO IT YOURSELF. THERE'S NO DANGER. TAKE SOME OF YOUR MEN ASHORE. DO THE JOB I WOULD HAVE DONE IF IT HADN'T BEEN FOR THAT MINE.

I'M ALMOST PERSUADED, CONNORS. IS THIS AMERICAN LIEUTENANT IMPORTANT ENOUGH FOR ME TO RISK THE LIVES OF MY MEN?

CONNORS INSISTED HE WAS, AND SOON MANAGED TO PERSUADE TONY WHO IMMEDIATELY CALLED THE CREW TOGETHER AND TOLD THEM WHAT HE HAD IN MIND.

MEN, I'M GOING ASHORE TO DO WHAT THE COMMANDOS WERE TO DO. I NEED FOUR MEN WITH ME. ANY VOLUNTEERS?

WE'RE WITH YOU, SIR!

ALMOST EVERY MEMBER OF THE TRENT'S CREW VOLUNTEERED. TONY COULD PICK THE BEST.

HE CHOSE PETTY OFFICER JIM FOX, AN EXPERIENCED SEAMAN, AND THREE RATINGS TO ACCOMPANY HIM. AS THEY PADDLED TOWARDS THE SHORE HE OUTLINED THE PLAN FOR FREEING THE AMERICAN OFFICER.

WHAT DO WE DO WITH THIS YANK WHEN WE'VE GOT HIM, SIR?

TURN HIM OVER TO CAPTAIN CONNORS, PETTY OFFICER FOX. THEN BACK TO ALEX, I SUPPOSE.

TWENTY MINUTES LATER THE FIVE NAVY MEN WERE LANDING IN HABBIBAH. THERE WAS NO SIGN OF LIFE IN THE SEEMINGLY-DESERTED PORT.

THE INHABITANTS ARE PROBABLY SHIVERING IN THEIR BEDS, WONDERING WHAT'S HAPPENING. WE HEAD FOR THE PRISON, AND MEET AN ITALIAN OFFICER NAMED BORTI.

PERHAPS THERE'LL BE THE CHANCE OF A FIGHT, SIR. NOT OFTEN WE GET TO MEET THE ENEMY FACE-TO-FACE.

THE GERMANS MIGHT HAVE LEFT HABBIBAH TO MEET THE THREAT ALONG THE COAST, BUT THE ITALIANS STILL GUARDED THEIR OWN PRIZE SEAPORT—AND AS TONY AND HIS MEN POUNDED A CORNER THEY CAME FACE TO FACE WITH AN ENEMY PATROL.

EYETIES, SIR. SHALL WE LET 'EM HAVE IT?

NO WAIT. LET'S GIVE 'EM A CHANCE TO SURRENDER!

TONY KNEW SOME ITALIAN AND SHOUTED TO THE SURPRISED SOLDIERS.

TONY'S WORDS WERE MET WITH A SUDDEN BURST OF GUNFIRE. THE ITALIAN PATROL MEANT TO SHOOT FIRST, AND ASK QUESTIONS LATER.

DOWN, MEN!

OPEN FIRE!

THE BRITISH BLASTED AWAY, BLANKETING THE ITALIANS WITH LEAD.

UP ON YOUR FEET, MEN. INTO 'EM, AND TAKE ONE ALIVE TO GUIDE US TO THE JAIL!

YOU HEARD THE CAPTAIN. INTO 'EM, LADS.

SHOUTING WILDLY, TONY LED HIS MEN IN A CHARGE UP THE STREET. THE ITALIANS RAN—ALL EXCEPT ONE WHO WAS NOT QUICK ENOUGH OFF THE MARK TO ESCAPE FROM PETTY OFFICER FOX.

GOT YOU, ME LAD!

GOOD MAN, PETTY OFFICER. HOLD HIM TIGHT!

THE DOOR OPENED AND MAJOR BORTI, WHO HAD BEEN AWAITING THE ARRIVAL OF THE BRITISH RAIDING PARTY, STOOD THERE. BUT THE NEWS HE HAD TO GIVE WAS BAD.

I AM MAJOR BORTI, COMMANDANTE OF THE PRISON. YOU ARE TOO LATE, INGLESI. THE AMERICAN IS NO LONGER HERE!

WHAT THE DEVIL ARE YOU ON ABOUT? THIS IS WHERE WE WERE SUPPOSED TO MEET HIM. IF YOU ARE BORTI YOU WERE BRIBED TO HAND HIM OVER.

TONY WAS ANGRY AND AS HE MENACED THE ITALIAN OFFICER, MAJOR BORTI SQUEAKED OUT THE NEWS THAT COOPER AND THREE BRITISH SOLDIERS WHO WERE IN THE JAIL WERE TAKEN ON BOARD A SHIP ONLY HOURS EARLIER TO BE TAKEN TO A PRISON CAMP IN ITALY.

THERE WAS NOTHING I COULD DO. IT WAS ON THE ORDERS OF THE GERMAN SECRET SERVICE WHO HAD INTERROGATED HIM.

WHAT SORT OF SHIP? A WARSHIP? A SUBMARINE? WHAT SHIP?

BACK ABOARD, TONY SNAPPED OUT ORDERS FOR THE SUB TO SET SAIL FOR DEEPER WATERS. THEN HE WENT TO SEE CONNORS WHO WAS STILL IN PAIN, TO TELL HIM THE BAD NEWS. THE COMMANDO MADE A SNAP DECISION—

YOU MUST GO AFTER THAT ITALIAN RED CROSS SHIP AND TAKE THE AMERICAN OFF, NEWMAN. YOU KNOW WHAT YOUR ORDERS WERE WHEN WE LEFT ALEX?

TO OBEY YOU UNTIL THE AMERICAN WAS SAFE ON BOARD. TO TELL YOU THE TRUTH, CONNORS, I'M GOING AFTER THAT FREIGHTER ANYWAY!

A COURSE WAS SET, AND THE SUB SAILED AT FULL SPEED ON THE SURFACE, A DANGEROUS THING TO DO DURING DAYLIGHT, BUT ESSENTIAL IF THE SUB WAS TO CATCH UP WITH THE ITALIAN FREIGHTER.

CORRECT COURSE, YOU THINK, TONY?

BORTI SAID SHE WAS BOUND FOR NAPLES, TERRY. THIS IS THE BEST WAY TO NAPLES I KNOW FOR A SHIP CARRYING THE RED CROSS!

THE RED CROSS SYMBOL INDICATED A HOSPITAL SHIP WHICH WOULD BE UNLIKELY TO BE ATTACKED.

A FEW HOURS AFTER DAWN TWO VESSELS WERE SPOTTED AND THE TRENT DIVED IMMEDIATELY.

WE'LL GO IN A BIT CLOSER FROM BELOW AND FIND OUT WHAT THEY ARE.

USING THE PERISCOPE, TONY SOON IDENTIFIED THEM.

WHAT ARE THEY, SIR? THE FREIGHTER AND TRAWLER FROM HABBIBAH?

YES, RIGHT THERE IN FRONT OF US. WE COULDN'T HAVE HOPED FOR A BETTER MEETING!

TONY PLANNED TO DEAL WITH THE ARMED TRAWLER FIRST. ONCE THAT VESSEL WAS OUT OF THE WAY HE COULD SAFELY SURFACE AND BOARD THE ITALIAN RED CROSS SHIP WITHOUT ANY DANGER TO HIS SUB, FOR THE ITALIAN SHIP WOULD NOT BE ARMED.

FIRE ONE—FIRE TWO!

AYE, AYE, SIR!

THE TWO TORPEDOES LEFT THE SUB'S BOW TUBES, AND SPED THROUGH THE WATER, RIGHT ON TARGET.

TORPEDOES RUNNING TRUE. LET'S HOPE THEY'RE NOT SPOTTED.

ONE MISSED, BUT ONE HIT WAS ALL THAT WAS NEEDED. THE RESULTING EXPLOSION TORE A GAPING HOLE IN THE GERMAN TRAWLER.

ACHTUNG. WE'VE BEEN HIT BY A TORPEDO!

OVER THE SIDE, QUICK. IT'S OUR ONLY CHANCE!

WITHIN SECONDS THE TRAWLER SLID BENEATH THE SEA AS HER CREW SWAM FOR THE FREIGHTER.

AS THE ITALIANS RESCUED THEIR GERMAN ALLIES FROM A WATERY GRAVE, TONY WAS PUTTING THE NEXT STAGE OF HIS PLAN INTO OPERATION, AS ONE SHARP-EYED ITALIAN NOTICED.

SIR, OVER ON THE PORT BOW. A SUBMARINE JUST COMING TO THE SURFACE!

SO THAT'S WHAT SUNK OUR ESCORT.

TONY LED AN ARMED PARTY IN TWO DINGHIES TO BOARD THE FREIGHTER. HIS SIGNALLER HAD RADIOED THE ITALIAN SHIP WARNING HER NOT TO USE HER WIRELESS UNDER THREAT OF BEING SHELLED.

REMEMBER, WE AREN'T OUT TO HURT ANYBODY. THAT SHIP IS PROBABLY FULL OF WOUNDED SOLDIERS. ALL WE WANT IS THE AMERICAN LIEUTENANT THEY'RE TAKING TO NAPLES.

WHEN TONY AND HIS MEN BOARDED THE SHIP THEY SOON FOUND THAT THE ITALIAN CAPTAIN HAD PLENTY TO SAY ABOUT WHAT WAS GOING ON.

I MUST PROTEST MOST STRONGLY. THIS VESSEL CARRIES THE RED CROSS. YOU ARE PIRATES, AND I WILL . . .

I HAVEN'T HARMED YOUR SHIP, AND I WON'T. ALL I WANT IS THE AMERICAN OFFICER YOU HAVE ABOARD AS A PRISONER. AH YES, AND THE THREE BRITISH SOLDIERS.

SUDDENLY THERE WAS A GUTTURAL SHOUT FROM THE BRIDGE WHERE THREE ARMED GERMANS STOOD.

GET OUT OF THE WAY. LEAVE THE ENGLANDERS TO US!

JERRIES, UP THERE, MEN. PROBABLY THE AMERICAN'S GUARDS. GET 'EM BEFORE THEY DOWN US!

AS BRITISH AND GERMANS OPENED FIRE, THE ITALIANS DIVED FOR COVER.

THE GERMAN GUARDS HAD NO INTENTION OF GIVING UP THEIR VERY IMPORTANT AMERICAN PRISONER WITHOUT A STRUGGLE.

GOOD SHOT, PETTY OFFICER. COME ON, FOLLOW ME. I WANT TO GET AS CLOSE AS I CAN TO THAT LOT!

YOU HEARD THE CAPTAIN. THOSE JERRIES DON'T SEEM TO REALISE YET THAT WE'VE TAKEN OVER THE SHIP, WE GOT TO EXPLAIN TO 'EM!

THE SKIRMISH WAS SHORT AND SHARP. THE GERMANS, S.S. MEN WHO HAD BEEN ENTRUSTED WITH THE TASK OF ESCORTING LIEUTENANT BRAD COOPER TO GERMANY, FOUGHT TO THE LAST.

I DON'T THINK WE'LL SEE ANY MORE HOSTILITY IN THIS SHIP. ARE YOU OK?

JUST A SCRATCH, SIR, NOTHING TO WORRY ABOUT.

AND WITH THE GERMANS OUT OF THE FIGHT, THE ITALIAN SKIPPER WAS ONLY TOO PLEASED TO CO-OPERATE.

AT TONY'S COMMAND, THE PRISONERS WERE BROUGHT UP ON DECK. COOPER WAS OBVIOUSLY VERY PLEASED TO BE FREE AGAIN, BUT THE THREE BRITISH SOLDIERS LOOKED DISTINCTLY UNHAPPY.

THE ROYAL NAVY! BOY, AM I GLAD TO SEE YOU GUYS!

PLEASED TO BE OF SERVICE. A NAVY SUB LOST YOU, ONLY RIGHT THAT A NAVY SUB SHOULD SAVE YOU. I'M TONY NEWMAN, SKIPPER OF THE TRENT OVER THERE.

RESCUERS AND RESCUED RETURNED TO THE SUB, ALLOWING THE ITALIAN FREIGHTER TO CONTINUE HER INTERRUPTED VOYAGE TO NAPLES—AFTER DESTROYING HER RADIO. AND IN THE DINGHY, TONY NOTICED THAT THE SOLDIERS WERE NOT HAPPY.

THOSE THREE IN THE OTHER BOAT DON'T SEEM TOO PLEASED ABOUT THEIR RESCUE, LIEUTENANT.

THEY'VE NO REASON TO BE. YOU'D BETTER KEEP A CLOSE WATCH ON 'EM.

THE AMERICAN WENT ON TO EXPLAIN THAT HE'D HEARD THAT THE THREE SOLDIERS HAD BEEN FACING CHARGES OF MURDERING A BRITISH N.C.O. WHEN THEY WERE TAKEN PRISONER BY A GERMAN LONG RANGE PATROL.

THEIR BRITISH GUARDS WERE KILLED IN AN AMBUSH BY THE KRAUTS. IF THEY GO BACK TO EGYPT THEY'LL STILL HAVE TO FACE A MURDER CHARGE, I RECKON.

I CAN SEE WHY THEY WOULD HAVE PREFERRED TO STAY WHERE THEY WERE AS PRISONERS OF WAR. MURDERERS, EH?

SO, WHEN THEY GOT BACK TO THE SUB, TONY HAD THE THREE SOLDIERS PUT UNDER GUARD IN THE FORWARD TORPEDO ROOM.

AND WHEN COOPER WAS TAKEN TO CONNORS, TONY AT LAST HEARD WHY AN AMERICAN HAD BEEN ON BOARD THE ILL-FATED SYREN.

THE SYREN WAS CARRYING A CASE OF FIVE MILLION DOLLARS IN DIAMONDS. MY JOB WAS TO DISTRIBUTE THEM.

DISTRIBUTE THEM TO WHOM?

COOPER CONTINUED . . .

TO DESERT TRIBES SO THAT THEY WOULD FIGHT ON THE ALLIED SIDE.

WHAT HAPPENED WHEN THE SYREN WAS SUNK?

SO IT SEEMED THAT THE GERMANS WOULD ALREADY BE ON THEIR WAY WITH SALVAGE EQUIPMENT TO GET THEIR HANDS ON THE DIAMONDS BUT AS COOPER FINISHED HIS TALE, TONY HAD AN IDEA—

HOW ABOUT US TAKING A FURTHER HAND IN THIS GAME?

YOU MEAN GO AFTER THAT KING'S RANSOM OURSELVES?

THAT WAS PRECISELY WHAT TONY DID MEAN, AND THE THREE WERE SOON AGREED. WITH COOPER'S HELP THEY PLOTTED A COURSE TO THE LOCATION OF THE SUNK BRITISH SUBMARINE.

IT WAS DIFFICULT TO KEEP THE SECRET IN SUCH A CONFINED SPACE, AND IT WAS NOT LONG BEFORE THE WORD WAS PASSED THROUGH THE TRENT THAT THEY WERE OFF ON THE TRAIL OF A FORTUNE OF DIAMONDS.

COURSE IT'S TRUE. I HEARD SPARKS AND THE GUNNERY OFFICER TALKIN' ABOUT IT. FIVE MILLION DOLLARS WORTH OF DIAMONDS SPARKS SAID.

BLIMEY, THINK WHAT I COULD DO WITH ALL THAT.

THE CAPTIVE SOLDIERS WERE LISTENING CLOSELY. THEIR LEADER, A LANCE-CORPORAL NAMED FRED JACKSON, GRINNED EVILLY AS HIS COMPANIONS IN CRIME, PRIVATES JOHN TIBBS AND HARRY SMITH, BEMOANED THEIR FATE.

ALL WE GOT TO LOOK FORWARD TO IS A FIRING SQUAD, EH JACKSON?

DON'T BE TOO SURE OF THAT, SMITHY. WHILE THERE'S LIFE THERE'S HOPE. AND WHAT COULDN'T WE DO SOMEWHERE IN SOUTH AMERICA WITH FIVE MILLION DOLLARS WORTH OF DIAMONDS!

SO THE THREE MEN BEGAN TO SCHEME.

USING TONY'S CHARTS, AND COOPER'S KNOWLEDGE, H.M.S. TRENT SAILED BACK TO THE LIBYAN COAST, AND WHEN THE SUB REACHED THE POSITION WHERE THE SYREN WENT DOWN, TONY OBSERVED THROUGH THE PERISCOPE THAT THE ENEMY WAS ALREADY SEARCHING FOR THE TORPEDOED SUBMARINE.

LOOKS LIKE THE EYETIES ARE BUSY.

AN ITALIAN SALVAGE SHIP, ESCORTED BY A GERMAN E-BOAT, HAD ALREADY BEGUN DIVING OPERATIONS IN THE AREA.

SO FAR THE ITALIANS HAD NOT BEEN SUCCESSFUL IN THEIR SEARCH BUT TIME WAS NOT VITAL, AND THE DIVERS INTENDED TO COMB THE AREA METHODICALLY UNTIL THEY FOUND THE WRECK ON THE SEA BED.

MAYBE TODAY WILL BRING SUCCESS. SHE HAS TO BE DOWN THERE SOMEWHERE.

I DON'T CARE IF IT TAKES A MONTH. THIS IS THE SORT OF JOB I LIKE, GUISEPPE.

TONY WAS NOT PERTURBED TO FIND THE ENEMY ALREADY TRYING TO LOCATE THE WRECK AND HE TOLD COOPER WHAT HE HAD SEEN.

AS WE DON'T HAVE ANY SALVAGE EQUIPMENT OF OUR OWN I'M HAPPY TO LET THE ITALIANS DO THE SEARCHING FOR US.

I FIGURE THEY'RE OFF COURSE, SKIPPER. THE SYREN WENT DOWN A LITTLE TO THE EAST OF HERE.

AND SO, ABOARD TRENT, A PLOT WAS HATCHED. THE SUB COULD NOT STAY IN THE AREA INDEFINITELY, SO IT WAS DECIDED TO GIVE THE ITALIANS A HELPING HAND WITH THE SEARCH. THE SUB SURFACED WELL OUT OF SIGHT THAT NIGHT WITH TONY READY TO LEAD A SMALL BOARDING PARTY.

STAY UNOBSERVED UNTIL WE GET BACK, TERRY. I DON'T KNOW HOW LONG IT WILL TAKE.

BE CAREFUL. YOU'RE TAKING A HECK OF A GAMBLE.

TONY, COOPER AND FOX, IN THEIR DINGHY, HEADED FOR THE ITALIAN SALVAGE VESSEL, INTENDING TO BOARD IT UNSEEN.

GET THE SALVAGE SHIP BETWEEN OURSELVES AND THE E-BOAT. EVEN IF THE EYETIES DON'T HAVE A WATCH ON DECK, THE GERMANS WILL BE SURE TO.

I CAN'T SEE ANYBODY ON DECK FROM HERE, SIR. I BET THEY'RE RELYING ON THE JERRIES TO WATCH OVER 'EM!

THE MATE EAGERLY TOLD HIS CAPTORS THAT THE CAPTAIN WAS BELOW IN HIS CABIN WITH THE GERMAN WHO HAD BEEN SENT FROM THE E-BOAT TO KEEP THE ITALIANS ON THEIR TOES. AND AS THEY REACHED THE DOOR HE SPOKE WORRIEDLY.

DO NOT SHOOT THE CAPTAIN, HE IS MY BROTHER. YOU CAN DO WHAT YOU LIKE WITH THE GERMAN!

NOBODY WILL BE SHOT PROVIDED THEY DO NOTHING STUPID. STAND BACK WHILE I OPEN THE DOOR.

TONY'S FOOT HIT THE DOOR, AND IT FLEW INWARDS TO REVEAL THE TWO MEN PLAYING CHESS AT THE TABLE.

HIMMEL, WAS IST?

NOT A SOUND OUT OF EITHER OF YOU OR I'LL SHUT YOU UP FOR GOOD!

THE GERMAN PETTY OFFICER WAS PUSHED INTO A CORNER BY FOX, AND THE TERRIFIED FIRST MATE EXPLAINED THE SITUATION TO THE CAPTAIN IN A TORRENT OF ITALIAN.

THEY ARE INGLESI RAIDERS, MY BROTHER. DO AS THEY SAY OR THEY WILL KILL US ALL. I FOUGHT THEM BRAVELY ON DECK, BUT THEY WERE TOO MANY FOR ME!

LET THEM CARRY ON CHATTING FOR A MINUTE. THEY'RE SCARING EACH OTHER MORE THAN WE COULD.

PLAYING ON THE FACT THAT THE CAPTAIN AND THE MATE WERE BROTHERS, TONY TOLD THEM THAT HE AND HIS MEN WOULD STAY IN THE CABIN WITH THE CAPTAIN AND THE GERMAN DURING THE DAY WHILE THE FIRST MATE SUPERVISED THE DIVING OPERATIONS.

WHEN THE CHEST OF DIAMONDS IS BROUGHT UP YOU WILL BRING IT TO THE CABIN, AND HAND IT OVER TO US. DO YOU UNDERSTAND ME?

SI, SI, SIGNOR, I UNDERSTAND.

THE DIVERS WENT DOWN WITHOUT A WORD OF PROTEST, AND ONE OF THEM SOON SPOTTED THE WRECK OF H.M.S. SYREN LYING ON THE SEA-BED.

THERE SHE IS! BUT HOW DID LUIGI KNOW?

ONE DIVER ENTERED THE SUBMARINE, AND MADE HIS WAY TO THE CAPTAIN'S QUARTERS WHERE HE QUICKLY FOUND THE BOX OF DIAMONDS. SOON HE WAS RETURNING.

I FOUND IT. NOW TO GET UP TO THE SURFACE AGAIN.

WHEN HE GOT THE BOX BACK ON BOARD, THE CREW'S CHEERS AT HIS SUCCESS WERE SILENCED BY THE MATE WHO WAS WAITING ANXIOUSLY.

WE'VE DONE IT. WE'VE BROUGHT UP THE TREASURE!

GIVE IT TO ME—I MUST GET IT DOWN TO THE CABIN AT ONCE!

THE MATE GRABBED THE CHEST FROM THE STARTLED DIVER AND RUSHED INTO THE CABIN TO GIVE IT TO THE BOARDING PARTY. TO HIM HIS BROTHER'S LIFE WAS WORTH A HUNDRED SUCH BOXES.

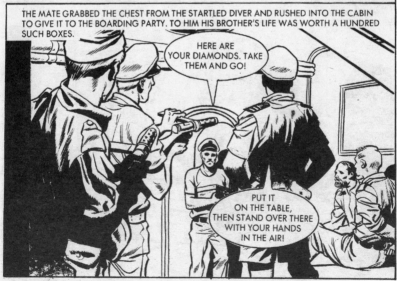

HERE ARE YOUR DIAMONDS. TAKE THEM AND GO!

PUT IT ON THE TABLE, THEN STAND OVER THERE WITH YOUR HANDS IN THE AIR!

FORCING THE LOCK WITH HIS KNIFE, TONY AND FOX STARED IN AMAZEMENT AT THE DIAMONDS.

BLIMEY, IT COULD MAKE A DISHONEST MAN OF YOU!

DON'T GET ANY IDEAS, PETTY OFFICER. THIS LOT GOES BACK TO ALEX.

TONY THEN TURNED TO LUIGI AND TOLD HIM WHAT WAS TO HAPPEN NEXT.

WE WILL LEAVE AT NIGHT AND TAKE YOUR BROTHER HOSTAGE. IF NO ALARM IS RAISED HE WILL BE RELEASED.

AND TO FOOL THE E-BOAT CREW THE DIVING WAS TO CONTINUE ALL DAY WITH THE ITALIAN CREW BEING TOLD THAT THERE WAS ANOTHER BOX TO BE RECOVERED.

BUT THOUGH THE RAIDERS HAD THE TWO ITALIANS COWED INTO SUBMISSION THE TIED-UP GERMAN WAS MADE OF STERNER STUFF AND SHOUTED ANGRILY.

YOU WILL PAY DEARLY FOR THIS, ITALIAN SCUM. WHEN I GET BACK TO THE GUARD BOAT—

YOU PIPE DOWN OR YOU WON'T BE GOING ANYWHERE, FRITZ. I COULD STILL PUT A BULLET IN YOU AND THROW YOU OVER THE SIDE!

FOX'S THREAT SHUT HIM UP.

AS SOON AS IT WAS DARK THE MATE CAME BELOW TO ADVISE THE THREE RAIDERS THAT IT WAS NOW SAFE TO LEAVE.

YOU COME WITH US, CAPTAIN. NO TRICKS, PLEASE.

FAREWELL, MY BROTHER. WE SHALL MEET AGAIN SOON—I HOPE!

AFTER CREEPING ACROSS THE DESERTED DECK THEY LAUNCHED THEIR DINGHY AND BEGAN TO PADDLE OFF. TONY HAD A FINAL WORD OF WARNING FOR THE MATE.

REMEMBER WHAT I SAID. SILENCE UNTIL WE SEND YOUR BROTHER BACK TO YOU!

IT WILL BE AS YOU SAY.

BUT WOULD IT? FOR AT THAT MOMENT THE WHOLE ENTERPRISE WAS ABOUT TO BE PUT IN JEOPARDY . . .

... BY THE SHIP'S COOK WHO WAS EVEN THEN TAKING A MEAL TO THE CAPTAIN'S CABIN.

HERE WE ARE, MI CAPITANO. SPAGHETTI . . .

GET RID OF THAT HOGWASH AND UNTIE ME, YOU DOLT!

AND BY THE TIME THE MATE ARRIVED BACK AT THE CABIN TO KEEP THE GERMAN QUIET THE DAMAGE HAD BEEN DONE—THE COOK HAD FREED HIM.

AND NOW WE MUST— SAPRISTI, WHAT IS GOING ON HERE?

OUT OF MY WAY!

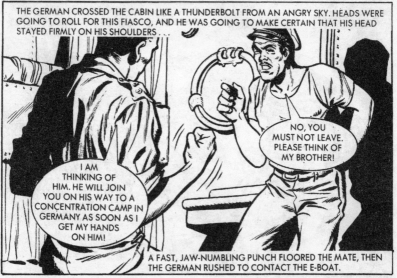

THE GERMAN CROSSED THE CABIN LIKE A THUNDERBOLT FROM AN ANGRY SKY. HEADS WERE GOING TO ROLL FOR THIS FIASCO, AND HE WAS GOING TO MAKE CERTAIN THAT HIS HEAD STAYED FIRMLY ON HIS SHOULDERS . . .

NO, YOU MUST NOT LEAVE. PLEASE THINK OF MY BROTHER!

I AM THINKING OF HIM. HE WILL JOIN YOU ON HIS WAY TO A CONCENTRATION CAMP IN GERMANY AS SOON AS I GET MY HANDS ON HIM!

A FAST, JAW-NUMBLING PUNCH FLOORED THE MATE, THEN THE GERMAN RUSHED TO CONTACT THE E-BOAT.

UNAWARE OF WHAT WAS HAPPENING ON THE SALVAGE SHIP, TONY AND HIS DIAMOND HUNTERS HAD REACHED THE TRENT. THE OCCUPANTS OF THE DINGHY WERE PULLED ABOARD.

HOW DID IT GO, TONY?

COULDN'T HAVE BEEN BETTER. TELL YOU ABOUT IT LATER, RIGHT NOW WE'VE GOT TO RETURN ONE SORROWING BROTHER TO ANOTHER.

TONY KEPT HIS PART OF THE BARGAIN, ALTHOUGH IF THE ITALIAN SALVAGE SKIPPER KNEW WHAT AWAITED HIM BACK ON HIS OWN VESSEL HE MIGHT NOT HAVE BEEN SO KEEN TO LEAVE THE SAFETY OF THE SUBMARINE.

GOOD LUCK. KEEP SWIMMING, YOU'LL SOON REACH YOUR SHIP.

WHEN WE MEET AGAIN I TOO WILL HAVE A GUN, INGLESI.

TONY AND HIS TWO COMPANIONS WERE CONGRATULATING THEMSELVES ON THE SUCCESS OF THEIR MISSION WHEN THE LOOKOUT ON THE BRIDGE SUDDENLY YELLED A WARNING.

THE JERRIES WILL FEEL PRETTY SICK WHEN THEY FOUND OUT WE'VE SNATCHED THE DIAMONDS FROM UNDER THEIR NOSES.

E-BOAT DEAD AHEAD. COMING IN AT TOP SPEED!

THE MEN ON THE BRIDGE LEAPT DOWN THROUGH THE HATCH, AND THE SUB CRASH-DIVED AS THE ENEMY CRAFT LAUNCHED TWO TORPEDOES.

SHE'S CRASH DIVING!

TORPEDOES RUNNING.

IT WAS GOING TO BE A CLOSE THING FOR THE TRENT.

THE TWO TORPEDOES PASSED HARMLESSLY ABOVE THE RAPIDLY DIVING SUBMARINE, MUCH TO THE DISMAY OF THE MEN OF THE E-BOAT WHO HAD BEEN MADE TO LOOK FOOLS BY THE RAIDERS FROM THE SUBMARINE.

DID WE SCORE A HIT?

NEIN, DUMKOPF!

EVERY AVAILABLE VESSEL WOULD NOW BE CALLED UPON TO HUNT THE BRITISH SUB TO PREVENT HER FROM RETURNING VICTORIOUS TO HER BASE WITH THE FORTUNE IN DIAMONDS.

IN H.M.S. TRENT, ALL HEARD THE SOUND OF THE E-BOAT'S ENGINES DIE AWAY, AND TONY CAREFULLY BROUGHT HIS SUB UP TO PERISCOPE DEPTH. THEN, AFTER A CAREFUL SCRUTINY OF THE SURFACE—

ANYTHING UP THERE, SIR?

NO WE'LL MOVE AS FAST AS WE CAN UNDERWATER, EAST ALONG THE COAST, TO EVADE ANY PURSUIT THEY SEND AFTER US.

ONCE ALL WAS SAFE, HE LEFT TERRY IN CHARGE AND WENT WITH COOPER TO SEE CAPTAIN CONNORS AND TELL HIM OF THEIR SUCCESS—AND COOPER HAD THE DIAMONDS TO SHOW HIM.

FIVE MILLION DOLLARS WORTH, CONNORS. I THINK WE'LL LEAVE THEM HERE IN YOUR CHARGE UNTIL WE REACH ALEX.

THEY'LL BE SAFE WITH ME. FOR WHAT YOU BOYS HAVE DONE I'M GOING TO RECOMMEND THAT YOU BE MADE HONORARY MEMBERS OF THE COMMANDOS.

WORD OF THE RECOVERY OF THE DIAMONDS SOON SPREAD THROUGHOUT THE BOAT. AND LANCE-CORPORAL JACKSON AND HIS FELLOW PRISONERS IN THE FORWARD TORPEDO ROOM HAD LISTENED EAGERLY TO ALL THE TALK.

MEDALS FOR EVERYBODY EXCEPT US. ALL WE CAN EXPECT IS A ROPE ROUND OUR BLOOMIN' NECKS.

DON'T YOU BE TOO SURE OF THAT, SMITHY. WHATEVER WE TRY WE GOT NOTHING TO LOSE.

SMITH AND TIBBS LEANED CLOSER AS JACKSON WHISPERED HIS PLAN . . .

... IF THEY RETURNED TO ALEXANDRIA THEY WOULD BE COURT-MARTIALLED, AND CERTAIN DEATH SENTENCES WOULD FOLLOW. SO WHY NOT MAKE A PLAY FOR THE DIAMONDS IN THE CAPTAIN'S CABIN? TIBBS HAD HIS DOUBTS, HOWEVER.

CRAZIER BETS HAVE PAID OFF IN THE PAST, TIBBS. AND IF WE CAN FORCE THIS SUB TO HEAD FOR A NEUTRAL PORT WE COULD END UP IN SOUTH AMERICA—RICH!

YOU MUST BE CRAZY, JACKSON. WE'D NEVER GET AWAY WITH IT. THREE BLOKES AGAINST THE CREW OF A WHOLE SUBMARINE?

WITH THE PROMISE OF FREEDOM AND WEALTH, TIBBS AND SMITH SOON AGREED.

THE NEXT DAY, AFTER A CAUTIOUS SCANNING OF THE HORIZON ALL ROUND, TONY DECIDED TO RUN ON THE SURFACE. THE SUB CAME UP FROM THE DEPTHS, AND A BRIDGE LOOKOUT WAS KEPT.

TEN DEGREES. RIGHT, I'VE GOT HER. GOOD GRIEF, IT LOOKS LIKE A SUB!

OVER THERE, TEN DEGREES TO PORT, SIR. SOME SORT OF VESSEL LYING CLOSE TO THE WATER!

AT THAT DISTANCE TONY WAS UNSURE WHETHER THE VESSEL WAS FRIEND OR FOE.

WE'LL KEEP MOVING AT FULL SPEED TOWARDS HER UNTIL WE'RE SURE WHAT SHE IS. BUT WE'LL BE READY FOR ACTION.

AS SOON AS HE RECOGNISED THE OTHER SUB, TONY GAVE THE COMMAND TO START SHOOTING.

SHE'S AN ITALIAN. OPEN FIRE!

FIRE!

AS TWO SHELLS STRADDLED HER, THE ITALIAN SUB BEGAN TO CRASH DIVE, BUT TONY WASN'T FINISHED YET.

FIRE!

WE'RE TOO LATE!

TONY ORDERED TRENT TO DIVE, INTENDING TO STALK THE ENEMY SUB UNDER THE WATER, FOR HE COULD NOT LEAVE HER FREE TO HUNT HIM ALL THE WAY TO ALEXANDRIA, AWAITING THE MOMENT TO SEND THEM TO THE BOTTOM WITH A WELL-AIMED TORPEDO.

LISTEN OUT FOR ANY SOUND OF HER. WE MIGHT GET A CHANCE TO RAM HER BELOW THE SURFACE!

SO BELOW THE MEDITERRANEAN WATERS, A DEADLY GAME OF CAT AND MOUSE WAS PLAYED WITH BOTH SUBS LISTENING INTENTLY FOR A SOUND FROM THE OTHER.

RIG FOR SILENT RUNNING. WE DON'T WANT THE EYETIES TO GET US BEFORE WE GET THEM.

IT WAS A GAME WHICH COULD END IN VICTORY FOR ONE—OR DISASTER FOR BOTH.

THEN TRENT FOUND HER TARGET AND TONY GUIDED HIS SUB IN ON A COLLISION COURSE WITH THE ENEMY VESSEL.

IT WAS A STRIKE, AND EVERYONE KNEW IT WHEN THE SUDDEN JAR SENT THEM SPRAWLING TO THE DECK. THE LIGHTS DIMMED FOR A MOMENT, THEN BRIGHTENED.

ALL OVER THE SUBMARINE THE RESULT WAS THE SAME. THOSE CREW MEMBERS WHO WEREN'T HOLDING ON TIGHT LOST THEIR BALANCE. THE RESULT WAS MOMENTARY CONFUSION AND IN THE FORWARD TORPEDO ROOM, JACKSON INTENDED TO MAKE GOOD USE OF THIS.

THIS IS THE CHANCE WE'VE BEEN WAITING FOR. LET'S GET OUT OF HERE. GET TO THE CAPTAIN'S QUARTERS!

THAT'S WHERE THAT COMMANDO OFFICER IS, WITH THEM DIAMONDS!

BARGING ACROSS THE FALLEN RATINGS, JACKSON AND HIS FELLOW MURDERERS ESCAPED FROM THE TORPEDO ROOM, AND SOON WERE OUTSIDE TONY'S QUARTERS.

WE ALL GO IN TOGETHER. THAT COMMANDO'S PROBABLY GOT A GUN ON HIM TO WATCH OVER THE LOOT WITH. AND HE WON'T BE SLOW TO USE IT!

IF HE TRIES TER USE IT ON ME, I'LL DEAL WITH HIM!

THE MURDERERS MADE THEIR MOVE. ONE QUICK LUNGE, AND THEY WERE THROUGH THE CURTAIN INTO THE CAPTAIN'S QUARTERS.

WHAT THE DEVIL'S THE MEANING OF THIS?

LOOK OUT, JACKSON, HE'S GOIN' FOR A GUN.

THOUGH WOUNDED AND SURPRISED, THE COMMANDO'S REFLEXES WERE STILL BATTLE-SHARP.

BUT HE WASN'T QUICK ENOUGH. JACKSON GRABBED HIS GUN HAND.

DROP IT. OR I'LL BREAK YOUR WRIST!

YOU CAN'T GET AWAY WITH THIS, YOU FOOL!

JACKSON WRENCHED THE GUN FROM CONNORS' HAND THEN KNOCKED HIM OUT.

THAT'S HIM FIXED! NOW GET LOOKING FOR THEM DIAMONDS . . .

THEN IT'S US FER SOUTH AMERICA!

WITH THE DUEL BETWEEN THE TWO SUBMARINES STILL GOING ON, JACKSON WAS SURE THEY WOULDN'T BE DISTURBED WHILE THEY SEARCHED. AND A COUPLE OF MINUTES LATER TIBBS FOUND THE BOX OF GEMS.

I GOT 'EM. HERE THEY ARE, JACKSON. GOSH, LOOK AT THESE BEAUTIES!

GOOD FOR YOU, TIBBS. NOW TO GET THAT LIEUTENANT NEWMAN BACK HERE. HE'LL HAVE TO OBEY OUR ORDERS FROM NOW ON, UNLESS HE WANTS THAT COMMANDO CAPTAIN TO WIND UP DEAD.

BUT THERE WAS NO NEED TO CALL TONY. THE ALARM HAD ALREADY BEEN RAISED FROM THE FORWARD TORPEDO ROOM THAT THE THREE MEN HAD ESCAPED AND ALREADY A SEARCH WAS ON.

WE'LL TRY EVERY ROOM BETWEEN HERE AND THE TORPEDO ROOM.

IT'S MY BET, THEY'RE AFTER THE DIAMONDS.

SO TONY, FOX AND COOPER RUSHED TO THE CABIN.

THE EX-PRISONERS HAD THE WHIP HAND, AND THEY KNEW IT, AS THEY TOLD TONY WHEN HE AND THE OTHERS REACHED THE CABIN.

WE'VE GOT YOUR COMMANDO OFFICER IN HERE, CAPTAIN, AND UNLESS YOU DO AS I SAY I'LL SHOOT HIM!

ARE YOU MAD? WE'RE UNDER THE WATER BEING STALKED BY AN ITALIAN SUB—IF WE DON'T GET HER FIRST EVERYONE WILL DIE!

JACKSON TOLD TONY TO CALL OFF THE UNDERWATER HUNT IMMEDIATELY, FOR HE WANTED TO BE TAKEN TO SPANISH MOROCCO AND LANDED UNHARMED ON THE COAST WITH TIBBS AND SMITH—AND THE DIAMONDS.

WE'LL KEEP CAPTAIN CONNORS WITH US, AND IF YOU TRY TO TRICK US WE'LL KILL HIM. WE'VE GOT NOTHING TO LOSE. THEY CAN ONLY SHOOT US ONCE!

ALL RIGHT. I'LL ORDER MY FIRST LIEUTENANT TO CALL OFF THE HUNT.

TONY DIDN'T LIKE BEING BLACKMAILED LIKE THIS, BUT HE KNEW THERE WASN'T MUCH HE COULD DO JUST THEN.

PANIC-STRICKEN, THE ITALIANS TRIED TO ESCAPE FROM THEIR DOOMED SUB.

MAMMA MIA!

THE SHOCK OF THE IMPACT WAS FELT ABOARD TRENT, AND IN THE CAPTAIN'S QUARTERS EVERYONE WAS FLUNG VIOLENTLY OFF THEIR FEET.

NOW'S MY CHANCE!

GET HIM, JACKSON!

WHEN THE ROLLING SUBSIDED, TONY HAD HIS HAND ROUND JACKSON'S GUN WRIST. THOUGH HE DIDN'T KNOW WHAT HAD CAUSED THE IMPACT HE WAS DETERMINED TO GET THE GUN OFF JACKSON AS THEY GRAPPLED.

GIVE UP, JACKSON. WHATEVER'S HAPPENED, YOU CAN'T WIN!

IF I CAN GET YOU I'LL BE SATISFIED.

TONY DECIDED TO SURFACE AND ON THE BRIDGE HE AND TERRY SURVEYED THE DAMAGE TO THE SUB CAUSED BY THE COLLISION.

AS H.M.S. TRENT SAILED PAST THE WRECKAGE OF THE ITALIAN SUBMARINE THEY REALISED HOW LUCKY THEY HAD BEEN.

AND WITH JACKSON, SMITH AND TIBBS SAFELY UNDER GUARD ONCE AGAIN, THEY WERE SOON ON COURSE FOR THEIR BASE.

# WARSHIPS OF WORLD WAR 2

## No. 49: SURCOUF (France): Submarine
### (Second largest sub during WW2)

Displacement 2880 tons surfaced,
4300 tons submerged. Length 110m (361 feet)
Speed 18 knots surfaced, 8.5 knots submerged.
Crew 118

Armament 4 bow-tubes
8 stern-tubes in two trainable mounts
22 torpedoes carried: 2 203mm (8-inch)
2 37mm (1 46-inch)
1 aircraft

## No. 50: I-400 (Japan): Submarine
### (Largest sub during WW2)

Displacement 5223 tons surfaced,
6560 tons submerged.
Length 122m (400.25 feet).
Speed 18.5 knots surfaced,
6.5 knots submerged.
Crew 144.

Armament 8 bow-tubes, 20 torpedoes carried
1 140mm(5.5-inch) 10 25mm (1-inch)
3 aircraft with 4 torpedoes
three 800kg bombs and eight 250kg bombs

# JAVA SEA JINX

**H.M.** SUBMARINE "JUNIPER'S" OPERATIONAL CAREER IN THE FAR EAST GOT OFF TO A GOOD START WITH PLENTY OF SUCCESSFUL RAIDS ON JAP SHIPPING, BUT ONE NIGHT SHE COLLIDED WITH A NATIVE FISHING BOAT — AND FROM THEN ON IT SEEMED THAT SHE WAS SET ON A COURSE TO DESTRUCTION!

A CHEER WENT UP FROM JUNIPER'S CREW AS SHE QUIVERED TO THE SHOCK-WAVES OF THE EXPLOSION.

IAN WAS RIGHT. A FEW DAYS LATER HE RECEIVED A SIGNAL FROM NAVAL HEADQUARTERS.

NEW SKIPPER'S COMIN' ABOARD IN AN HOUR, SIR. TWO AN' A HALF RINGER, NAME OF DRURY.

LIEUTENANT— COMMANDER MICHAEL DRURY, EH? I DON'T KNOW HIM, HE MUST HAVE ARRIVED WHILE WE WERE ON PATROL...

JUNIPER'S CREW WAITED EAGERLY FOR THE NEW SKIPPER, FOR THEIR LIVES MIGHT DEPEND ON HIS ABILITY.

HE LOOKS A TOUGH CHARACTER. LET'S HOPE HE ISN'T A SLAVE–DRIVER.

WELL, THEY WOULDN'T GIVE US A PEN-PUSHER. I WONDER WHERE HE SERVED BEFORE HE CAME TO CEYLON?

ONCE ABOARD, DRURY INFORMED IAN THAT HE HAD BEEN SERVING IN THE MEDITERRANEAN WAITING FOR A COMMAND AND HAD BEEN POSTED TO THE FAR EAST AT SHORT NOTICE.

...SO I DON'T KNOW ANYTHING ABOUT THE JAPS, BUT I'M LOOKING FORWARD TO FINDING OUT.

LET'S HOPE WE DON'T HAVE TO WAIT TOO LONG, SIR. WOULD YOU LIKE TO INSPECT THE CREW NOW?

DURING THE PARADE, IAN HAD AN UNCOMFORTABLE FEELING THAT SOMETHING WAS WRONG.

WHAT'S UP WITH THE LADS? THEY DON'T SEEM VERY PLEASED.

THEY'RE WARY BECAUSE THEY DON'T KNOW ANYTHING ABOUT HIM. THEY'LL SOON SETTLE DOWN.

WHEN DRURY CAME TO ABLE SEAMAN WILLY TINDALE HE WAS MET WITH A HARD STARE AND WHEN ASKED HIS NAME, WILLY REPLIED IN A COLD VOICE. THE NAME SEEMED FAMILIAR TO DRURY.

TINDALE, EH? HAVE YOU ANY RELATIVES IN THE NAVY?

I HAD A BROTHER. HE WAS LOST WITH YOUR LAST COMMAND — SIR!

THERE WAS AN UNCOMFORTABLE SILENCE, THEN THE NEW SKIPPER MOVED ON.

I'LL SEE TINDALE AFTER THE PARADE, NUMBER ONE. I'D LIKE TO TALK TO HIM ABOUT HIS BROTHER.

SO THAT'S THE TROUBLE — WILLY MUST HAVE TOLD THE OTHERS ALL ABOUT IT...

WHILE HE WAS WAITING FOR WILLY, DRURY EXPLAINED THAT HIS LAST COMMAND HAD BEEN SUNK BY GERMAN BOMBERS IN THE ATLANTIC.

WE WERE SURFACED, AND A FEW OF US GOT OFF AS SHE WENT DOWN. TINDALE'S BROTHER WAS WITH US, AND WE SPENT SEVERAL DAYS ADRIFT IN A DINGHY.

BUT I THOUGHT HIS BROTHER WAS KILLED, SIR?

THEY ALL DIED OF EXPOSURE — THE ATLANTIC IS MERCILESS IN WINTER. I WAS THE ONLY SURVIVOR.

AND WILLY OBVIOUSLY THINKS THE SKIPPER SAVED HIMSELF AT THE EXPENSE OF THE OTHERS...

FROM THEIR ATTITUDE, IT LOOKED AS IF THE CREW HAD ALL HEARD WILLY'S VERSION — AND BELIEVED IT.

AFTER THE INTERVIEW WITH WILLY TINDALE, DRURY ADMITTED TO IAN THAT IT HAD BEEN A WASTE OF TIME.

HE STILL BLAMES ME FOR HIS BROTHER'S DEATH.

IT'S A PITY, SIR. HE'S ONE OF OUR BEST MEN.

IAN COULD SEE TROUBLE AHEAD, FOR THERE WAS NO ROOM FOR ILL-FEELING IN A SUBMARINE.

PERHAPS WE COULD POST WILLY TO ANOTHER SHIP, SIR.

NO, THAT WOULD LOOK AS IF I'VE SOMETHING TO HIDE.

IT WAS AN UNWISE DECISION, FOR WILLY WAS NOT THE FORGIVING TYPE. BUT WHILE HE BROODED, PLANS WERE GOING AHEAD FOR ANOTHER OPERATIONAL PATROL — BUT A PATROL WITH A DIFFERENCE, INVOLVING A SMALL COMMANDO UNIT —

WE'RE TAKING CAPTAIN RAILE AND TWO MEN AS PASSENGERS, AND WE'RE DROPPING THEM ASHORE ON AN ISLAND IN THE JAVA SEA.

A CLOAK AND DAGGER JOB, SIR?

VIC RAILE EXPLAINED THAT HE AND HIS MEN WERE GOING TO LIAISE WITH GUERILLAS.

I'M AFRAID YOU CHAPS WILL HAVE TO BRING US HOME AGAIN, BUT WE'LL TRY NOT TO KEEP YOU WAITING.

SO LONG AS YOU DON'T WANT US TO GO ASHORE WITH YOU, SIR. I DON'T FANCY CREEPING AROUND IN THE JUNGLE.

IT WAS AN UNWELCOME TASK, FOR THE SUBMARINE WOULD BE AT A DISADVANTAGE IN COASTAL WATERS.

LOTS OF RISK AND LITTLE REWARD ON THIS SORT OF OPERATION. THE JAP COASTAL PATROLS ARE HOT STUFF!

WE CERTAINLY SHAN'T GET MUCH CHANCE TO USE OUR TORPEDOES. AND THIS WEATHER ISN'T GOING TO HELP...

RIGHT FROM THE START BAD WEATHER PUT JUNIPER WELL BEHIND SCHEDULE.

TAKING ADVANTAGE OF PATCHY FOG, THEY FORGED AHEAD.

AS JUNIPER SLOWED, THE SWIRLING FOG CLEARED BRIEFLY TO REVEAL ANOTHER SHIP COMING TOWARDS THEM.

ENEMY DESTROYER TO STARBOARD, SIR!

BELAY THOSE ORDERS, NUMBER ONE, THE JAPS HAVE SEEN US!

AN OLD MAN WAS CLINGING DESPERATELY TO JUNIPER'S BOWS, BUT THERE WAS NO TIME TO HELP HIM OR THE OTHER SURVIVORS AS THE JAPANESE SHIP ATTACKED.

AAIIEE, HELP ME!

DIVING STATIONS — THOSE NIPS ARE GETTING CLOSE WITH THEIR SHELLS.

UNABLE TO DEPRESS HIS GUNS SUFFICIENTLY, THE JAPANESE SKIPPER WAS STILL CONFIDENT OF A KILL — BY RAMMING THE JUNIPER.

WITH A DESPAIRING WAIL THE OLD MALAYAN WAS SWEPT FROM JUNIPER'S BOWS AS SHE DIVED.

WE'RE TOO CLOSE TO SHOOT!

WE CAN STILL CUT THEM IN TWO. THEY CAN'T ESCAPE!

AAAGHHHH!

AND IN THE NICK OF TIME JUNIPER PLUNGED BENEATH THE WAVES. A SECOND LATER AND SHE WOULD HAVE BEEN SLICED IN HALF BY THE DESTROYER.

CURSE THEM, THEY'VE GOT AWAY! STAND BY DEPTH-CHARGES!

JUNIPER WAS SAFE FOR THE MOMENT, BUT DRURY WAS CERTAIN THAT THE ENCOUNTER WOULD NOT END THERE.

ENRAGED BY THEIR FAILURE, THE JAPANESE RETURNED AND SHOWERED THE AREA WITH DEPTH-CHARGES. THEY WERE DETERMINED THAT THE JUNIPER WOULD NOT ESCAPE THEM AGAIN AND THEY GAVE NO THOUGHT FOR THE REFUGEES IN THE WATER WHO WERE KILLED BY THE CONCUSSION.

IAN CALMLY REASSURED THE YOUNGSTER BUT THE SITUATION WAS GROWING DESPERATE.

ISN'T THERE ANYTHING MORE WE CAN DO?

I'VE TRIED EVERY TRICK IN THE BOOK. EXCEPT ONE...

DRURY HESITATED — THEN HE HAD A TORPEDO TUBE LOADED WITH SOME CURIOUS ITEMS...

THE JAP DINGHY AND CAP, THOSE OLD OVERALLS.

IT WAS THE VERY MATERIAL THEY HAD SALVAGED FROM THE JAP SUB THEY HAD SUNK IN THE UNDERWATER DUEL.

AFTER THE NEXT LOT OF DEPTH-CHARGES, THE WHOLE LOT WAS BLOWN OUT OF THE TORPEDO TUBE TO RISE TO THE SURFACE AND JUNIPER PUMPED OUT SOME FUEL OIL, TOO.

WE'VE GOT THEM, THERE'S OIL RISING!

THEY CAN'T FOOL US WITH THAT OLD TRICK. I'LL BELIEVE IT IF THERE ARE ANY BODIES...

BUT THE JAPANESE SMILES FADED SWIFTLY WHEN THEY RECOGNISED THE CAP AND DINGHY.

IT'S AN IMPERIAL NAVY DINGHY — SUBMARINE ISSUE!

AND AN OFFICER'S CAP — WE'VE SUNK ONE OF OUR OWN SUB-MARINES!

FAR BENEATH THE SURFACE, JUNIPER'S CREW WAITED AND LISTENED TO THE ACTIVITY ABOVE THEM AS THE JAPS LOOKED FOR MORE EVIDENCE.

THEY'VE SEARCHED AROUND FOR HALF AN HOUR, BUT IT SOUNDS AS IF THEY'RE MOVING OFF.

THEY CERTAINLY WON'T FIND ANY SURVIVORS! BUT IT'S TIME WE WERE MOVING, TOO...

THE DARK BROODING OVER HIS BROTHER'S DEATH HAD MADE HIM DETERMINED TO RUIN DRURY.
HE SPUN A CONVINCING TALE —

THE OLD BLOKE CLINGING TO THE BOWS CURSED US AS HE WAS SWEPT AWAY. I WAS ON THE BRIDGE, AND I HEARD HIM!

BLIMEY, I WONDER IF THAT'S WHY WE WERE CLOBBERED? HE PUT THE EVIL EYE ON US...

THE SAILORS, TENSE AND ILL–AT–EASE AFTER THEIR ORDEAL, READILY BELIEVED THIS STORY.

THAT NIGHT HE INTENDED TO CONTINUE HIS CAMPAIGN TO TURN THE CREW AGAINST DRURY.
AS HE STOOD ON THE BRIDGE ON LOOKOUT...

THEY BELIEVED THAT BIT ABOUT THE CURSE, BUT I RECKON IT NEEDS A GHOST TO MAKE IT MORE CONVINCING...

WHEN HE WENT OFF WATCH, HE CLAIMED TO HAVE SEEN A GHOST ON THE SHADOWY DECK. ALFIE CRAIG WAS AMONGST THOSE WHO BELIEVED EVERY WORD.

IT WAS THAT OLD BLOKE, ALL MISTY AND WITH GLARING EYES. AND HE POINTED AT THE SKIPPER.

COR, LET'S HOPE I DON'T SEE HIM. I'D BE SCARED STIFF!

WILLY WAS CLEVER ENOUGH NOT TO REPORT THE "GHOST" TO THE OFFICERS. THEY WOULD HAVE SEEN THROUGH HIS PLAN AND HE WOULD HAVE BEEN IN SERIOUS TROUBLE.

THE NEXT NIGHT WHEN CRAIG WAS ON LOOKOUT WITH IAN...

AAGHHH!

WHAT'S WRONG WITH YOU, CRAIG?

IAN KNEW THAT YOUNGSTERS LIKE ALFIE WERE NERVOUS AND EASILY INFLUENCED.

I SAW A GHOST, SIR. THAT OLD MAN WHO DROWNED AFTER THE COLLISION!

NONSENSE, IT WAS MIST. THERE'S NOTHING THERE.

YOUNG ALFIE CRAIG'S STORY WAS SOON ALL ROUND THE SUBMARINE, AND WILLY TINDALE USED IT RUTHLESSLY TO INFLUENCE THE CREW.

THE FOLLOWING NIGHT THEY SLIPPED INTO THE JAVA SEA AND PREPARED TO DROP THEIR COMMANDO PASSENGERS AT THE ISLAND.

VIC AND HIS TWO TRUSTED SERGEANTS, NED BARKER AND JIM MILLER, PADDLED ASHORE ON THEIR DANGEROUS MISSION. MINUTES LATER JUNIPER WAS HEADING OUT TO SEA.

IT'S A PITY WE'VE GOT TO WASTE THREE DAYS WAITING AROUND FOR FOR THE SOLDIERS, SIR.

WE SHAN'T WASTE THEM, NUMBER ONE. I'VE GOT PERMISSION TO DO SOME HUNTING.

JUNIPER SUBMERGED, AND IN THE CONTROL ROOM DRURY EXPLAINED THAT SO LONG AS THEY STAYED AWAY FROM THE COAST, THEY COULD HUNT FOR JAPS.

WE'LL PATROL THESE SHIPPING LANES AND TRY OUR LUCK. IT'S TIME WE TOOK THE OFFENSIVE.

AND A FEW SUCCESSES MIGHT HELP MORALE, SIR. YOUNG CRAIG'S GHOST HAS MADE EVERY-ONE JUMPY.

IAN HAD PUT DOWN THE GHOST TO THE YOUNGSTER'S OVER-ACTIVE IMAGINATION. HE KNEW NOTHING OF WILLY TINDALE'S EFFORTS TO SPREAD RUMOURS.

AT FIRST IT SEEMED THAT THEIR LUCK HAD CHANGED, FOR THE NEXT DAY THEY SIGHTED SOME SMALL JAPANESE COASTERS.

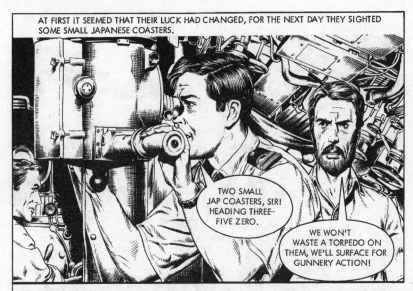

TWO SMALL JAP COASTERS, SIR! HEADING THREE—FIVE ZERO.

WE WON'T WASTE A TORPEDO ON THEM, WE'LL SURFACE FOR GUNNERY ACTION!

JUNIPER SURFACED SMOOTHLY AND THE GUN CREW SPRINTED TO THEIR ACTION STATIONS. THE FIRST SHELL BURST ALONGSIDE THE LEADING STEAMER.

UP ONE HUNDRED! RAPID FIRE!

TWO HUNDRED FEET BELOW THE WAVES, JUNIPER SETTLED ON THE BOTTOM AS MORE BOMBS RAINED DOWN.  SHE HAD SUFFERED ENOUGH DAMAGE TO CAUSE CONCERN.

THERE'S A PRESSURE LEAK, SIR. AND THERE IS SOMETHING WRONG WITH THE PUMPS!

THEY COULD FEEL NO MORE EXPLOSIONS.  IN THE CONTROL ROOM IAN AND DRURY DISCUSSED THE DAMAGE.

I'M AFRAID REPAIRS WILL TAKE AT LEAST AN HOUR, SIR.  BUT THE AIRCRAFT HAS GONE.

LET'S HOPE IT DOESN'T COME BACK WITH ANY PALS. WE'RE STUCK HERE UNTIL THOSE PUMPS ARE WORKING.

AND WHILE THEY LAY HELPLESS, WILLY TINDALE WAS STIRRING UP MORE ILL-FEELING AGAINST THE SKIPPER.

NOW I KNOW DRURY'S A JINX. I'M PUTTING IN FOR A TRANS- FER AS SOON AS WE GET BACK.

GOOD IDEA, MATE, I DON'T FANCY MAKIN' A MEAL FOR THE FISHES. MAYBE WE SHOULD ALL APPLY.

IAN, GOING FORWARD TO CHECK ON THE PROGRESS OF REPAIRS, OVERHEARD THE END OF THE CONVERSATION.

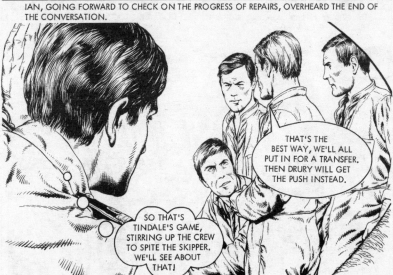

THAT'S THE BEST WAY, WE'LL ALL PUT IN FOR A TRANSFER. THEN DRURY WILL GET THE PUSH INSTEAD.

SO THAT'S TINDALE'S GAME, STIRRING UP THE CREW TO SPITE THE SKIPPER. WE'LL SEE ABOUT THAT!

SOON IT WAS TIME TO HEAD FOR THE ISLAND AGAIN, TO PICK UP VIC RAILE AND HIS MEN.

COAST IN SIGHT, SIR. DO YOU WANT TO GO ANY CLOSER?

NO, WE'LL LIE LOW UNTIL NIGHT–FALL AND THEN MOVE IN ON THE SURFACE.

SOON AFTER DARK THEY SURFACED AND HEADED FOR THEIR RENDEZVOUS WITH VIC AND HIS MEN.

HAVE THE GUN CREW STAND BY, NUMBER ONE. IF WE'RE CAUGHT IN THE SHALLOWS WE'LL HAVE TO FIGHT.

THE GUN'S OUT OF ACTION, SIR. THAT BOMBING DAMAGED THE ELEVATING MECHANISM.

WHEN IAN CAME BELOW WITH CHIEF PETTY OFFICER BENNETT, THEIR CALL FOR VOLUNTEERS MET WITH AN UNEASY SILENCE.

I DON'T KNOW WHAT'S GOT INTO 'EM, SIR. BUT I'LL SOON DETAIL A CREW...

DON'T BOTHER, CHIEF, I'D SOONER GO ALONE THAN WITH UNWILLING CONSCRIPTS WHO MIGHT LET ME DOWN!

FROM IAN'S TONE OF VOICE IT WAS OBVIOUS THAT HE DIDN'T THINK MUCH OF THE MEN.

STILL ANGRY, IAN PREPARED TO GO OFF ALONE. HE CLIMBED OUT OF THE DECK HATCH AND GOT INTO THE WAITING DINGHY. DRURY SAW HIM FROM THE BRIDGE AND WONDERED WHY HE WAS ALONE.

WHAT'S HAPPENING, NUMBER ONE?

I'M GOING ON MY OWN, SIR. I SHAN'T BE LONG.

ONCE IAN WAS OFF ON HIS HAZARDOUS TASK C.P.O. BENNETT TOLD THE SAILORS EXACTLY WHAT HE THOUGHT OF THEM.

HE DIDN'T GIVE US TIME, CHIEF. WE WOULDN'T HAVE REFUSED TO GO...

I HOPE YOU'RE PROUD OF YOURSELVES! LIEUTENANT CHADWICK'S GONE ON HIS OWN — IF IT'S A TRAP HE WON'T STAND A CHANCE.

MOST OF THEM FELT ASHAMED AT NOT HAVING VOLUNTEERED. ONLY WILLY STILL SEEMED DEFIANT, BUT AFTER THE CHIEF'S WORDS HE, TOO, BEGAN TO FEEL GUILTY.

MEANWHILE IAN WAS ROWING STEADILY TOWARDS THE SHORE — AND THE MYSTERIOUS LIGHT.

TOO LATE TO TURN BACK NOW. IF THE JAPS ARE THERE THEY COULDN'T MISS ME AT THIS RANGE!

HE WAS RELIEVED WHEN NED BARKER CAME STUMBLING DOWN THE BEACH.

WHERE ARE THE OTHERS?

I'LL TELL YOU ON THE WAY BACK. LET'S GO, THERE ARE JAPS ABOUT!

BARKER EXPLAINED THAT HIS TWO COMPANIONS HAD BEEN CAPTURED BY THE JAPS AND WERE BEING HELD IN THE JAPANESE CAMP.

WE BUMPED INTO A JAP PATROL THIS AFTERNOON AND THEY WERE GRABBED. LUCKILY I WAS LAGGING BEHIND AND THE JAPS DIDN'T SEE ME.

THAT'S BAD NEWS. THEY CAN'T HAVE TALKED, OR THE JAPS WOULD HAVE BEEN WAITING FOR US.

IT LOOKED AS IF THE JAPS MIGHT HAVE BEEN TAKEN IN BY THE SOLDIERS' COVER STORY.

WE WERE TOLD TO SAY WE'D BEEN LIVING IN THE AREA WITH THE NATIVES SINCE THE JAP INVASION, SIR.

IF THEY BELIEVE THAT, THE JAPS MIGHT NOT BE SO TOUGH ON YOUR MATES. BUT IT'S A SLIM CHANCE...

THERE SEEMED LITTLE CHANCE OF HELPING THE PRISONERS, BUT IAN WAS WILLING TO TRY.

BARKER FOLLOWED THE JAPS TO THEIR CAMP, SIR, AND HE COULD LEAD US BACK THERE.

IT'S TOO LATE TO TRY ANYTHING TONIGHT, AND IF THOSE TWO MENTION THE SUB-MARINE WE COULD FIND OURSELVES TRAPPED HERE...

DRURY KNEW THE SAFETY OF JUNIPER AND HER CREW CAME FIRST. BUT HE COULD NOT SIMPLY ABANDON THE PRISONERS.

ALL RIGHT, YOU WIN. WE'LL RETURN TOMORROW AT DUSK AND YOU CAN TAKE A PARTY ASHORE.

THANKS, SIR, WE'LL DO OUR BEST. I'D BETTER GET SOME PLANS WORKED OUT.

BARKER TOLD IAN ALL HE COULD ABOUT THE JAPANESE CAMP AND SURROUNDING JUNGLE AND TOGETHER THEY WORKED OUT THE BEST WAY TO FREE THE PRISONERS.

THIS TIME WHEN A SHORE PARTY WAS NEEDED THERE WAS NO SHORTAGE OF VOLUNTEERS. EVEN WILLY TINDALE STEPPED FORWARD.

I THOUGHT YOU'D GOT IT IN FOR THE FIRST LIEUTENANT, MATE!

HE'S GOT GUTS, CHUM — SO IF HE'S GOING ASHORE AGAIN I'M GOING WITH HIM.

WILLY AND HIS MATE "PINCHER" MARTIN WERE ACCEPTED IMMEDIATELY, FOR THEY WERE THE BEST SHOTS ON BOARD.

CHANGED YOUR MINDS, HAVE YOU? MAKE SURE YOU DON'T LET JUNIPER DOWN WHEN YOU GET ASHORE.

YOU KNOW US, CHIEF. IF THEM NIPS WANT A SCRAP WE'LL GIVE THEM ONE!

THE FOLLOWING NIGHT IAN AND HIS MEN ROWED ASHORE AND LANDED ON THE DESERTED BEACH. ALL THE A.B.s HAD PUT ON OVERALLS AND WOOLLEN CAPS TO MERGE WITH THE DARKNESS.

BETWEEN THE BEACH AND THE JAP CAMP LAY A WIDE STRETCH OF SWAMPY JUNGLE.

IAN HAD BROUGHT A COMPASS, AND A DRUM OF THIN CORD THAT THEY UNWOUND AS THEY ADVANCED.

IF WE COME BACK IN A HURRY WE'LL NEED A MARKER. NOBODY WILL NOTICE THE CORD. MOST OF IT WILL BE UNDER WATER.

IT WAS SLOW GOING, FOR SEVERAL TIMES THEY HAD TO SKIRT BAD PATCHES, BUT BY DAWN THE SWAMP WAS BEHIND THEM.

CUT THE CORD AND TIE IT TO THIS TREE, SO WE CAN FIND IT AGAIN. AND HIDE THE DRUM.

WE'LL PUT IT UNDER THESE BUSHES, SIR.

WITH THEIR ESCAPE ROUTE SECURED, THEY MOVED ON WITH NED BARKER GUIDING THEM.

THAT'S THE PLACE, SIR. BUT I WASN'T ABLE TO SEE WHERE THE JAPS TOOK OUR BLOKES.

WE'LL NEED TO KNOW EXACTLY WHERE THEY ARE BEFORE WE GO IN AFTER THEM.

THE JAPANESE CAMP WAS LARGER THAN IAN HAD EXPECTED, AND IT WAS GUARDED.  THERE WAS NO CHANCE OF A SUCCESSFUL RELEASE DURING DAYLIGHT.

HOURS PASSED WITH NO SIGN OF THE PRISONERS — THEN PINCHER SUDDENLY SAW VIC RAILE.

AND AS IAN WATCHED HE COULD SEE MILLER BEING BROUGHT OUT OF THE SAME HUT.

VIC HAD NO IDEA THAT FRIENDS WERE SO NEAR, AS HE AND HIS COMPANION WERE MARCHED OFF FOR INTERROGATION.

I RECKON THIS IS IT, SIR. I DON'T THINK I CAN STAND ANOTHER BEATING UP...

SILENCE! NO TALK UNTIL ASKED QUESTION!

THEY WERE BROUGHT BEFORE THE COLONEL IN CHARGE OF THE CAMP WHO HAD SOME UNPLEASANT NEWS FOR THEM.

I NO BELIEVE YOUR STORY, BUT I HAVE FINISH WITH YOU! TOMORROW COME OFFICERS OF THE KEMPI TAI. THEY MAKE YOU TELL TRUTH!

THEN IF WE CAN'T ESCAPE TONIGHT, WE'VE HAD IT!

VIC HAD NO DOUBT OF THEIR FATE AT THE HANDS OF THE KEMPI TAI — THE DREADED JAPANESE SECRET POLICE.

AS DARKNESS FELL, TWO SAILORS CREPT STEALTHILY TOWARDS THE FAR SIDE OF THE CAMP AND WATCHED A SENTRY'S EVERY STEP.

HE'S MOVING OFF, NOW'S OUR CHANCE!

THRUSTING THEIR HOME-MADE BOMBS INTO THE THATCH, THEY LIT THE FUSES AND WITHDREW HURRIEDLY.

WHEN THOSE FIRES TAKE HOLD THEY'LL JUMP FROM ONE ROOF TO THE NEXT.

WE'D BETTER NOT BE AROUND. COME ON!

WITH A MUFFLED ROAR, THE DRY THATCH BURST INTO FLAMES — TO THE HORROR OF THE JAPANESE SOLDIERS.

AAIIEE, FIRE!

SOME FOOL MUST HAVE LIT A COOKING FIRE IN HIS HUT!

AS THE JAPS RUSHED TO EXTINGUISH THE FLAMES, IAN WENT AHEAD WITH HIS PLANS.

ACCOMPANIED BY WILLY AND PINCHER, IAN HURRIED INTO THE CAMP AND MADE FOR THE PRISON HUT.

THE PRISONERS SOON FORGOT THEIR DISCOMFORT AS THEY GRABBED THE RIFLES FROM THE TWO JAPANESE GUARDS.

UNFORTUNATELY ONE OF THE INCENDIARIES HAD FAILED TO BURN AND WAS DISCOVERED, LEADING ONE OFFICER TO THE RIGHT CONCLUSION.

THE JAPANESE OFFICER IMMEDIATELY ORDERED A CHECK ON THE PRISON HUT.  AND WHEN THEY SAW THE TWO GUARDS LYING THERE...

AND AS IAN AND HIS COMPANIONS HURRIED THROUGH THE SHADOWS THERE WAS A SHOUTED CHALLENGE.

THE FIRING DREW JAPS FROM EVERY DIRECTION, AND THE FUGITIVES WERE SOON IN DANGER OF BEING CUT OFF FROM THEIR ESCAPE ROUTE.

BY THIS TIME THE TWO FIRE-RAISERS HAD REJOINED NED BARKER AND HIS TWO COMPANIONS.

REJOINING BARKER AND THE OTHERS, THEY HURRIED INTO THE WELCOMING JUNGLE.

THEY WON'T FIND US IN THIS LOT!

IAN'S FORESIGHT PAID OFF WHEN THEY FOUND THEIR CORD MARKER AND BEGAN TO FOLLOW IT.

THAT'S A SMART IDEA! BUT WHAT IF THE JAPS FOLLOW IT?

IT'S BEING ROLLED UP BEHIND US!

AND ALTHOUGH THE JAPS STARTED TRIUMPHANTLY IN PURSUIT, THEY WERE SOON IN TROUBLE.

AAAIIEEE, HELP ME — I'M SINKING!

THEY MUST HAVE CROSSED HERE. BUT HOW COULD THEY FIND THEIR WAY IN THE DARKNESS?

IAN'S "ROPE TRICK" BAFFLED THE JAPANESE SOLDIERS.

BY THE TIME IAN AND HIS COMPANIONS REACHED THE BEACH THERE WAS NO SOUND OF PURSUIT.

COR, IT'S ALL OVER BAR THE TRIP HOME!

DON'T COUNT YOUR CHICKENS, MATE. WE'RE NOT ON BOARD YET!

WITH THE FIGHTING OVER, WILLY HAD REVIVED HIS GRIEVANCE AGAINST JUNIPER'S SKIPPER, AND AS HIS WOUND WAS BANDAGED HE BEGAN TO COMPLAIN TO IAN.

YOU RECKON DRURY WILL COME IN FOR US WHEN HE KNOWS WE'VE STIRRED UP THE JAPS?

MY SIGNAL'S JUST BEEN ANSWERED, AND A BOAT'S ON ITS WAY!

BUT DRURY STILL HAD AN ACE TO PLAY.  SWINGING JUNIPER'S BOWS TO FACE THE JAP—HELD ROCK HE FIRED TWO TORPEDOES.

BLIMEY, THE ONLY SUBMARINE EVER TO TORPEDO AN ISLAND!

THE FORCE OF THE EXPLODING TORPEDOES SHOOK THE ROCK AND SENT THE JAP MACHINE GUN TUMBLING INTO THE SEA.

AAAGHHH!

BY THIS TIME SOME COASTAL GUNS HAD JOINED IN THE ACTION, AND JUNIPER WAS UNDER HEAVY FIRE.

LOOKS AS IF WE'VE STIRRED UP A HORNET'S NEST, SIR!

THEN WE'LL MOVE IN CLOSER AND HURRY THINGS ALONG.  A BIT MORE RISK WON'T MAKE MUCH DIFFERENCE!

ONCE EVERYONE WAS SAFELY ON BOARD, DRURY TOOK JUNIPER OUT OF THE SHALLOWS TO DEEP WATER WHERE SHE COULD SUBMERGE. BELOW DECKS, WILLY MADE HIS POSITION CLEAR.

BUT IT WAS YOU SAID THE SKIPPER WOULD LAND US IN TROUBLE...

LOOK, MATE, IF DRURY HADN'T BROUGHT THE OLD TUB INSHORE, WE'D HAVE BEEN SHARK-BAIT BY NOW!

AS WILLY CONTINUED TO SING DRURY'S PRAISES IAN CAME UP NOISELESSLY BEHIND HIM.

I KNOW I WAS AGAINST DRURY, BUT I'VE CHANGED MY MIND. HE'S GOT WHAT IT TAKES!

I DON'T THINK THE SKIPPER WILL HAVE ANY MORE TROUBLE WITH WILLY TINDALE!

AND A FEW MINUTES AFTER THEY SUBMERGED CAME FINAL PROOF THAT JUNIPER WAS
LUCKY AS IAN, ON PERISCOPE WATCH, SPOTTED A NEW TARGET.

THERE'S A JAP DESTROYER APPROACHING, SIR. THEY MUST HAVE SEEN THE FIRES ON SHORE!

GOOD JOB WE'VE RELOADED THE BOW TUBES. ALL RIGHT, NUMBER ONE, I'LL TAKE HER!

DRURY CHANGED COURSE, GOT THE RANGE OF THE DESTROYER AND GAVE THE ORDER TO FIRE.

TWO WELL-AIMED TORPEDOES SENT THE JAP DESTROYER TO A WATERY GRAVE.

AAAGHH!

ANY DOUBTS THE CREW HAD HAD ABOUT DRURY WERE NOW DISPELLED. AS FAR AS THEY
WERE CONCERNED, JUNIPER WAS A LUCKY SHIP.

WITH HER MISSION COMPLETED AND THREE NEW KILLS ON HER SCOREBOARD, JUNIPER HEADED TRIUMPHANTLY FOR CEYLON. FOR THE REST OF THE WAR SHE OPERATED FROM THERE WITH GREAT SUCCESS, BUT NOBODY EVER CLAIMED TO HAVE SEEN THE OLD MAN'S GHOST AGAIN — NOT EVEN WILLY!

Commando
THE END

# WARSHIPS OF WORLD WAR 2

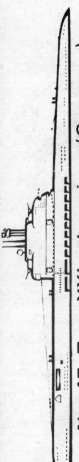

## No. 47: Type XXI submarines (Germany)

Displacement 1621 tons surfaced, 1819 tons submerged. Length 72.2m(237 feet). Speed 15.5 knots surfaced, 5 knots submerged with electric motors running silent or 17 knots for one hour only with full electric power. Crew 57.
Armament—6 tubes in bow, 23 torpedoes carried or 12 torpedoes and 12 mines. 4 20mm(0.79-inch).

## No. 48: T-Class submarines (Britain)

Displacement 1090 tons surfaced, 1570 tons submerged. Length 74.8m(245.5 feet). Speed 15 knots surfaced, 9 knots submerged. Crew 56.
Armament—8 tubes in bow, 1 in stern, 2 amidships firing forward at an angle. 16 torpedoes carried: 1 102mm(4-inch). 3 7.6mm(0.303-inch) machine guns.

# DIVE! DIVE! DIVE!

H.M.S. TAMARIN WAS PATROLLING AT PERISCOPE DEPTH OFF THE COAST OF NEW GUINEA WHEN LIEUTENANT DICK CRASKE SIGHTED A JAPANESE SUBMARINE ON THE SURFACE. THERE WAS NO TIME TO WASTE AS HE SENT THE CREW SPEEDING TO ACTION STATIONS . . . FOR THE ENEMY CRAFT WAS RUNNING SILENTLY ON HER ELECTRIC MOTORS AND HAD PROBABLY ONLY SURFACED BRIEFLY TO SEND A WIRELESS MESSAGE, TAKING ADVANTAGE OF THE VERY POOR VISIBILITY.

WITH A HOLLOW RUMBLE AND A WHOOSH OF AIR, THE SLEEK TORPEDOES WERE LAUNCHED . . .

. . .RUNNING SILENTLY TOWARDS THEIR DOOMED TARGET.

FOR WHAT FELT LIKE AN AGE, IT SEEMED THEY HAD MISSED — TILL, SUDDENLY, TAMARIN SHUDDERED.

WE GOT 'EM, SIR!

OF COURSE! STAND BY TO SURFACE.

AFTER SURFACING TO LOOK FOR SURVIVORS, A SEARCH PRODUCED ONLY A FEW BITS OF FLOATING DEBRIS.

JUST BITS OF A WOODEN BOX, SIR. NO MARKINGS OF ANY KIND ON THEM.

PITY. IT'S NICE TO HAVE SOME EVIDENCE, ALTHOUGH I DON'T THINK H.Q. WILL WANT PROOF.

TRAVELLING SURFACED FOR GREATER SPEED DESPITE THE WEATHER, TAMARIN ALTERED COURSE TO MAKE THE RENDEZVOUS.

EVEN IF THIS IS A SUCCESS I'LL BE KNOWN AS THE CHAP WHO SANK THE ANGELFISH.

THAT NIGHT, WHEN THEY MADE CONTACT WITH A JAP AIRCRAFT, DICK CALLED PETER TO THE BRIDGE.

WE SAW HIM ON THE RADAR, BUT HE DISAPPEARED.

HE MAY BE UP TO SOMETHING. MAKE SURE YOU ALL STAY ALERT.

PETER'S INSTINCTS SERVED HIM WELL — FOR SUDDENLY ONE OF THE LOOKOUTS RAISED THE ALARM.

AIRCRAFT ON PORT BOW, SIR ...ATTACKING!

DICK DIDN'T FEEL CONFIDENT, BUT HE TRIED NOT TO LET IT SHOW. HE KNEW HOW EASILY THE MISSION COULD GO WRONG, AND SO DID THE SAILORS WITH HIM.

HOW DO WE KNOW THE JAPS AIN'T CAUGHT OUR AGENTS, SIR, AND FORCED 'EM TO GIVE ALL THE RENDEZVOUS DETAILS?

WE DON'T, WHICH IS WHY THE SUB'S STANDING BY OUT THERE TO GIVE US COVERING FIRE IF WE NEED IT.

THEY HAD NO CAUSE TO WORRY AS MAJOR STEVE JARROW STEPPED OUT OF THE GLOOM, ACCOMPANIED BY ABU, HIS INDONESIAN GUIDE.

WE'RE JOLLY GLAD TO SEE YOU, BUT WE THOUGHT THE YANKS WERE COMING TO PICK US UP?

A TECHNICAL HITCH, SIR, BUT I'LL TELL YOU ABOUT IT LATER. YOU'D BETTER HOP ABOARD BEFORE WE'RE NOTICED.

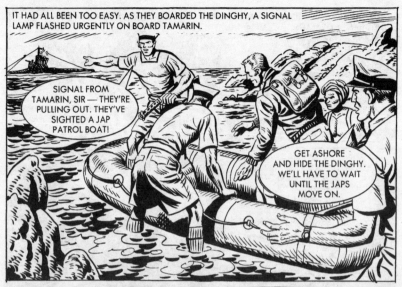

IT HAD ALL BEEN TOO EASY. AS THEY BOARDED THE DINGHY, A SIGNAL LAMP FLASHED URGENTLY ON BOARD TAMARIN.

SIGNAL FROM TAMARIN, SIR — THEY'RE PULLING OUT. THEY'VE SIGHTED A JAP PATROL BOAT!

GET ASHORE AND HIDE THE DINGHY. WE'LL HAVE TO WAIT UNTIL THE JAPS MOVE ON.

THE MAJOR LOOKED ANXIOUS AS HE WATCHED THE SUBMARINE MOVE SILENTLY OUT TO SEA.

THEY SHOULD HAVE WAITED. WE'RE CARRYING DOCUMENTS VITAL TO ALLIED INTELLIGENCE!

THEY'LL BE BACK WHEN THE JAPS HAVE GONE.

BY THE TIME TAMARIN REACHED DEEP WATER AND COULD SUBMERGE, THE JAPANESE SHIP WAS DANGEROUSLY CLOSE.

NOW DICK HAD TIME TO TELL THE MAJOR ABOUT THE LOSS OF ANGELFISH, THE CHANGE OF PLANS.

MAYBE THAT ACCOUNTS FOR THOSE EXPLOSIONS I HEARD OFF SUBARIA.

SUBARIA? THAT ISLAND A FEW MILES OFF THE COAST?

THE AGENT'S STORY OF WHAT HAD SOUNDED LIKE A DEPTH-CHARGE ATTACK BY A FLYING BOAT OFFERED A LIKELY EXPLANATION TO THE FATE OF THE U.S.S. ANGELFISH . . .

. . . THE TIMING WAS RIGHT, AS THE FIRST RENDEZVOUS DATE HAD BEEN THE NIGHT TAMARIN HAD ATTACKED AND SANK WHAT THEY ALL HOPED HAD BEEN A JAP SUBMARINE. IT WOULD STILL TAKE MORE THAN SOMEBODY'S WORD TO CLEAR DICK'S CONSCIENCE, THOUGH.

HOWEVER STEVE'S REPORT AS THEY CROUCHED IN COVER HAD CHEERED HIM UP AND WHEN THE JAPANESE DEPARTED AFTER ONLY A FEW MINUTES, THE BRITISH SUB SURFACED WITHOUT FURTHER INTERRUPTION.

WELCOME ABOARD, WE'LL TRY AND MAKE YOU BOTH AT HOME. SORRY ABOUT THE DELAY.

NO NEED TO APOLOGISE. WE'RE ONLY TOO GLAD TO BE ON OUR WAY.

AFTER MAKING HIS PASSENGERS COMFORTABLE, DICK TOLD PETER ABOUT WHAT HAD POSSIBLY HAPPENED TO THE ANGELFISH.

COULD WE MAKE A SMALL DETOUR ON THE WAY BACK, SIR? THERE MAY BE SURVIVORS ON SUBARIA — IT HAS A JAP GARRISON.

FAIR ENOUGH, SO LONG AS WE DON'T ENDANGER THE MAJOR AND HIS DOCUMENTS. THEY HAVE PRIORITY.

ALTHOUGH THE CHANCE OF FINDING SURVIVORS WAS SLIM, THEY MADE A THOROUGH SEARCH OF THE SEA AROUND THE ISLAND.

LOOKS AS IF WE'VE WASTED OUR TIME, SIR. I SUPPOSE IT WAS TOO MUCH TO HOPE FOR.

NEVER MIND, DICK. WE'LL FIND SOME SORT OF PROOF.

THE FOLLOWING MORNING, PETER AGREED TO A FINAL CHECK OF SUBARIA'S COAST.

WE'RE CLOSE ENOUGH TO SEE ANY SIGNS OF SURVIVORS BUT THE PLACE STILL LOOKS DESERTED.

THERE WERE PLENTY OF JAPS AROUND THE PORT AS WE CAME PAST. SORRY, DICK, BUT WE'LL HAVE TO ABANDON THE SEARCH.

THEY CLOSED THE HATCH AFTER SLIPPING INTO THE CONNING TOWER.

NOW DICK COULD OPEN THE LOWER HATCH WITHOUT FEAR OF FLOODING THE SUBMARINE.

LUCKILY THERE WAS NO WATER IN THE CONTROL ROOM. THEIR TORCHES REVEALED NOTHING UNUSUAL—UNTIL DICK REMOVED HIS MASK.

CHLORINE! KEEP YOUR MASK ON. THE HULL'S FULL OF GAS.

THE KILLER GAS, GENERATED BY THE ACTION OF SALT WATER ON THE BATTERIES, MADE DICK CHOKE AS HE TRIED TO REPLACE HIS BREATHING APPARATUS.

FORTUNATELY HE SOON RECOVERED ONCE HE HAD REPLACED HIS MOUTHPIECE. A SEARCH OF THE BOAT REVEALED TWO DEAD MEN IN THE ENGINE ROOM.

. . . BOTH GASSED BEFORE THEY COULD REACH THEIR MASKS.

BUT THIS STILL DIDN'T EXPLAIN HOW THE OTHERS HAD MANAGED TO GET AWAY.

WITH THEIR OXYGEN SUPPLY RUNNING LOW, THEY DECIDED TO RETURN TO TAMARIN.

BETTER CLOSE THE HATCH, ALTHOUGH I DON'T SUPPOSE IT MATTERS.

AS THEY WERE ABOUT TO LEAVE HOWEVER, DICK'S COMPANION GRABBED HIM BY THE ARM AND POINTED INTO THE DISTANCE WHERE A LARGE CREATURE WAS POWERING THROUGH THE WATER.

A CROCODILE! IT'S ALMOST AS BIG AS A LIFEBOAT!

HARDLY DARING TO BREATHE, BOTH MEN HID AS THE HUGE SALT-WATER CROCODILE SWAM PAST WITHOUT NOTICING THEM.

IT MUST BE FIFTEEN FEET LONG, AT LEAST. OUR KNIVES WOULDN'T EVEN SCRATCH IT.

AS SOON AS IT HAD DISAPPEARED FROM VIEW THEY SWAM HURRIEDLY BACK TO THEIR SUBMARINE.

SAFELY BACK ON BOARD, DICK TOLD PETER ALL THAT HAD HAPPENED.

APART FROM THE TWO DEAD MEN, IT LOOKS AS IF THE WHOLE CREW GOT AWAY. THEY MUST BE ON SHORE.

THE JAPS WOULD HAVE CAUGHT THEM BY NOW. THE ISLAND ISN'T THAT BIG, AND THERE'S QUITE A LARGE JAP GARRISON.

AT LEAST NOW THEY KNEW THE SUB THEY HAD SUNK WAS JAPANESE — THAT WAS A WEIGHT OFF DICK'S MIND.

WHEN STEVE HEARD DICK'S STORY, WHILE RELAXING IN THE WARDROOM, HE IMMEDIATELY OFFERED TO GO ASHORE AND FIND OUT WHAT HAD HAPPENED TO THE AMERICANS.

WE CAN'T LET YOU DO THAT, SIR. I'D BE COURT-MARTIALLED IF ANYTHING HAPPENED TO YOU.

OKAY, THEN LET ABU GO. HE USED TO LIVE ON SUBARIA BEFORE THE WAR. HE STILL HAS FRIENDS THERE.

ABU, STEVE'S INDONESIAN COMPANION, BEAMED AT THE PROSPECT OF BEING PART OF THE MISSION.

AS SOON AS IT WAS DARK, THEY SURFACED AND THE DINGHY WAS LAUNCHED. DICK, FEELING RESPONSIBLE FOR THE PARTY'S SAFETY, VOLUNTEERED HIS SERVICES.

I'D LIKE TO GO WITH THEM, SIR, JUST TO MAKE SURE NOTHING GOES WRONG.

ALL RIGHT, BUT STAY WITH THE DINGHY AND WAIT. I DON'T WANT YOU SEEN WITH ABU.

PETER WAS RIGHT. IF ABU WAS SEEN WITH A BRITISH OFFICER, IT WOULD BLOW HIS COVER.

THREE HOURS HAD PASSED BY THE TIME ABU RETURNED. HE WAS PLEASED TO SEE DICK STILL WAITING FOR HIM.

WE HAD COMPANY A LITTLE WHILE AGO. A JAP PATROL CAME PAST.

YES. THEY PASS THROUGH VILLAGE WHILE ABU THERE.

RETURNING TO THE SUBMARINE, ABU TOLD THEM WHAT HE HAD LEARNED. THE CREW OF ANGELFISH WERE BEING HELD PRISONER BY THE JAPANESE IN THEIR ISLAND GARRISON.

WE HAVEN'T ENOUGH MEN TO STAGE A RESCUE. THE JAP TROOPS OUTNUMBER US AT LEAST TEN TO ONE SO THERE'S NOTHING WE CAN DO.

BUT FRIENDS ALSO SAY YANKEE SAILORS MOVE TOMORROW BY SEA TO JAP HEAD-QUARTERS.

THIS GAVE DICK AN IDEA. IN THE OPEN SEA, THE SUB WOULD HAVE THE ADVANTAGE OVER THE JAP SHIPS.

AS SOON AS HE WAS BACK ON BOARD, HE OUTLINED HIS PLAN TO PETER. THE TWO MEN PUT THEIR HEADS TOGETHER.

ABU SAID THERE ARE SOME ESCORT SHIPS IN PORT, BUT THE AMERICANS WILL BE ON BOARD A STEAMER.

WE CAN HANDLE THE ESCORTS IF WE TAKE THEM BY SURPRISE. WE COULD TAIL THEM UNTIL OUT OF SIGHT OF LAND.

THE NEXT MORNING, THE AMERICAN PRISONERS WERE MARCHED FROM THEIR TEMPORARY CAMP ONTO A STEAMER, GUARDED BY JAPANESE TROOPS.

MOVE, YANKEE DOG!

WITH THE AMERICANS ON BOARD, THE CONVOY SET SAIL.

TWO ESCORTS, BOTH WELL-ARMED. OUR PLAN WILL STILL WORK.

THE BRITISH WERE READY AND WAITING.

TURNING AWAY FROM THE SCATTERED DEBRIS, PETER WAS
SURPRISED TO SEE THAT THE STEAMER WAS LISTING BADLY.

I RECKON THE JAPS HAVE DECIDED TO SINK THEMSELVES, SIR, RATHER THAN LOSE FACE.

WE'VE GOT TO GET ALONGSIDE BEFORE SHE GOES DOWN OR WE'LL NEVER HAVE TIME TO PICK UP ANY SURVIVORS.

HE KNEW JAP AIRCRAFT BASED IN NEW GUINEA WOULD HAVE
BEEN ALERTED AND WERE PROBABLY ON THEIR WAY ALREADY,
SEEKING REVENGE.

MEANWHILE, ON BOARD THE STEAMER, THE LAST JAPANESE
RESISTANCE HAD BEEN OVERCOME AND THE PRISONERS
RELEASED. THE YANK SAILORS COULD HARDLY CONTAIN
THEMSELVES.

IT'S THE LIMEYS!

THE STEAMER'S GOING DOWN UNDER OUR FEET. IF TAMARIN ISN'T ALONGSIDE SOON, WE'LL BE DROWNED.

DESPITE THE DANGER AS THE SHIP ROLLED STILL FURTHER, PETER BROUGHT HIS COMMAND ALONGSIDE. THE TRANSFER BEGAN.

GET CRACKING. WE CAN'T STAY HERE MUCH LONGER. THE SHIP'S GOING UNDER.

AFTER A SPEEDY CHECK OF THE HOLD, DICK SWAM FOR HIS LIFE AS THE DOOMED STEAMER SLIPPED SILENTLY BENEATH THE SURFACE.

STEVE WAS ON HAND TO HELP HIM ON TO THE CASING.

WELL DONE. I COULDN'T HAVE ORGANISED A BETTER BOARDING PARTY MYSELF!

THANKS! YOU CAN HAVE THE NEXT ONE!

DICK BARELY HAD TIME TO REPORT TO PETER WHEN ONE OF THE LOOKOUTS SHOUTED A WARNING OF APPROACHING AIRCRAFT.

ANOTHER COUPLE OF MINUTES AND THEY'LL CATCH US.

DON'T WORRY. WE'LL BE ON OUR WAY BY THE TIME THEY GET HERE.

MINUTES LATER, THE JAP BETTY BOMBERS BEGAN THEIR ATTACK—BUT THEIR TARGET WAS ALREADY SUBMERGING.

THE HULL CREAKED AND GROANED AS THE DEPTH-CHARGES ERUPTED, ALTHOUGH NONE WERE NEAR ENOUGH TO DO ANY DAMAGE.

ONCE BENEATH THE SURFACE THE EXPLOSIONS DIED AWAY—BUT THE HUNT WAS NOT OVER YET. THE BRITISH OFFICERS KNEW WHAT WAS HAPPENING.

THEY'LL BE CIRCLING NOW, WAITING . . .

. . . AND EXPECTING US TO HEAD FOR HOME. WE'LL FOOL THEM BY STAYING PUT.

HE GAVE THE ORDER TO BOTTOM OUT.

HIS PLAN WORKED, FOR ALL WAS NOW QUIET AS THE SUB LAY MOTIONLESS ON THE OCEAN FLOOR.

GOOD. THEY'VE GIVEN UP. NOW IT'S TIME TO QUIZ THE AMERICANS.

THERE WERE STILL SOME QUESTIONS PETER NEEDED ANSWERED.

ONCE THEY WERE UNDER WAY AGAIN, DICK WAS SURPRISED TO LEARN THAT TED MOSKY WAS TEMPORARILY IN COMMAND OF THE CREW OF THE AMERICAN SUB. HE ASKED WHY.

OUR SKIPPER WAS KILLED BEFORE THE JAPS CAPTURED US. I GUESS IF IT WASN'T FOR YOU GUYS, OUR LIVES WOULDN'T BE WORTH A BENT NICKEL.

WELL, WE'LL TRY TO MAKE YOU COMFORTABLE ON BOARD. WOULD YOU MIND TELLING US JUST WHAT HAPPENED ON SUBARIA?

TED BEGAN HIS STORY. ANGELFISH HAD BEEN TRAVELLING FAST ON THE SURFACE IN BRIGHT MOONLIGHT.

THERE'S AN AIRCRAFT ON RADAR, CAPTAIN. IT'S ALMOST OUT OF RANGE, AND VERY HIGH.

THEY WATCHED THE AIRCRAFT BLIP CAREFULLY, BUT IT SOON PASSED, EVENTUALLY DISAPPEARING OFF THE RADAR SCREEN. TED AND THE CAPTAIN MOVED UP TO THE BRIDGE TO COLLECT THEIR THOUGHTS.

I GUESS IT WAS JUST A ROUTINE PATROL. GOOD JOB THE JAPS DON'T SEE SO GOOD. MOST OF 'EM WEAR SPECS!

YEAH, AND THEY HAVEN'T GOT RADAR. IF THEY DID WE'D BE IN TROUBLE BY NOW.

OVER-CONFIDENCE IN THE STRENGTH AND POWER OF THEIR SUBMARINE WAS THE AMERICANS WEAKNESS. THEY LACKED THE EXPERIENCE TO KNOW SOMETHING WAS GOING ON.

SO THE ATTACK CAME AS A SHATTERING SURPRISE. THE JAPANESE FLYING BOAT HAD DIVED TO SEA LEVEL BEYOND THE HORIZON BEFORE APPROACHING UNDER COVER OF DARKNESS AND BELOW THE RADAR.

HOLY SMOKE! A JAP!

GET BELOW! DIVING STATIONS!

CAUGHT TOTALLY UNPREPARED, THE SUB TOOK THE FULL FORCE OF THE ATTACK.

BUT IT LOOKED AS IF THIS WAS HER LUCKY NIGHT. NONE OF THE DEPTH-CHARGES HAD EXPLODED TOO CLOSE . . .

. . . THOUGH THE JAPS WERE KNOWN FOR NOT GIVING UP EASILY.

JUST AFTER ANGELFISH SUBMERGED, THE FLYING BOAT MADE A SECOND PASS TO RELEASE THE LAST OF HER DEADLY CARGO.

AS CHARGES EXPLODED ALL AROUND HER SHE ROLLED TO AND FRO, BUT AS THE NOISE DIED DOWN A HOLLOW, METALLIC THUD ECHOED THROUGH THE HULL.

WITH THE SUB SAFELY MOORED AS PLANNED, THE SKIPPER DECIDED NOT TO RISK THE LIVES OF HIS CREW BY KEEPING THEM ON BOARD. HE SENT MOST OF THEM ASHORE FOR SAFETY.

AREN'T YOU COMING WITH US, SIR?

NO, I'LL STAY HERE UNTIL THE JOB'S DONE. I'VE KEPT A SKELETON CREW SO WE CAN DIVE IF WE HAVE TO.

IT WAS WELL THOUGHT OUT — THEY COULD SIT ON THE SEA-BED AND HIDE WITHOUT SETTING OFF THE DEPTH-CHARGE.

LATER, WHEN TED RETURNED TO THE BEACH TO WATCH THE BOMB EXPERTS BEGIN WORK, HE WAS ALARMED TO SEE THE SUB START TO DIVE.

HECK, THEY'RE SUBMERGING! I GUESS THE SKIPPER'S NERVOUS ABOUT AIRCRAFT.

A JAP PLANE HAD PASSED HIGH OVERHEAD WITHOUT SEEING THE INTRUDERS.

ANOTHER CRISIS HAD DEVELOPED ON BOARD. AN ENGINEER STAGGERED INTO THE CONTROL ROOM, GASPING.

HELP . . . BATTERIES LEAKIN' . . .

THE BATTERIES NEAR THE ENGINE ROOM HAD STARTED TO LEAK POISONOUS CHLORINE GAS.

AS THE DEADLY VAPOUR SWIRLED INTO THE CONTROL ROOM, THE SKIPPER KNEW HE ONLY HAD MOMENTS IN WHICH TO ACT.

HE NEEDS FRESH AIR. GET HIM TO THE HATCH, QUICK!

I'LL GET IT OPEN, SIR!

AGAIN, INEXPERIENCE HAD CAUSED THE SKIPPER TO PANIC. WITHOUT THINKING, HE GAVE THE ORDER TO ABANDON SHIP—BUT SOON REGRETTED IT.

OH, NO! WHERE ARE THE OTHERS? THEY MUST STILL BE ON BOARD!

HE WAS RIGHT. THE TWO DEAD MEN DICK FOUND IN THE SUB WERE THE ENGINEER'S MATES — BUT THEY HAD DIED EVEN BEFORE HE HAD RAISED THE ALARM. .

AS THEY SWAM FOR SHORE THERE WAS A SWIRL OF WATER AS A DARK SHAPE LAUNCHED ITSELF AT THE SKIPPER.

AAAGHHH!

A CROCODILE!

FORTUNATELY ONLY ONE CROCODILE HAD ATTACKED. AS TED LISTENED TO THE SURVIVORS' STORIES, HE FACED A DIFFICULT DECISION.

WE GOT NO MASKS, BUT THERE'S A FEW GUNS, AND THE JAPS DON'T KNOW WE'RE HERE . . .

HE SENT A MAN TO CONTACT THE LOCAL NATIVES AND SEE IF THEY HAD ANY BOATS. THE SAILOR SOON RETURNED.

I FOUND ONE WHO SPEAKS ENGLISH, SIR, BUT HE SAYS THEY'VE ONLY SMALL FISHING BOATS.

NEVER MIND. WE CAN STILL SEND A FEW GUYS FOR HELP. LET'S HOPE THE LOCALS KEEP QUIET.

BUT THE NATIVE WHO HAD " HELPED " THEM WAS AN INFORMER AND HAD LED THE JAPS TO WHERE THE AMERICANS WERE HIDING. THE GAME WAS UP.

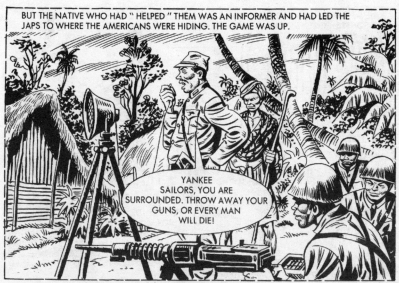

YANKEE SAILORS, YOU ARE SURROUNDED. THROW AWAY YOUR GUNS, OR EVERY MAN WILL DIE!

RESISTANCE WOULD HAVE BEEN POINTLESS. THEY HAD NO CHOICE BUT TO SURRENDER—BUT TED WARNED HIS MEN NOT TO GIVE ANYTHING AWAY.

I GUESS WE'RE LUCKY TO BE ALIVE, SIR.

YEAH, BUT THEY AIN'T GONNA GET ANGELFISH. LET THEM THINK SHE SANK OUT TO SEA AND WE CAME ASHORE BY DINGHY.

THEY ALL KNEW THE DAMAGE THE JAPS COULD DO IF THEY GOT THEIR HANDS ON AN ENEMY SUB. POSING AS AMERICANS, THERE WAS NO TELLING WHAT THEY WOULD GET UP TO.

THE JAPANESE HADN'T BOTHERED TO INTERROGATE THEIR PRISONERS, SO TED'S STORY HAD BEEN BELIEVED.

I GUESS THE STAFF AT NAVAL H.Q. WANTED US ALL TO THEMSELVES, SO THEY TOLD THE LOCAL HEAVIES TO LAY OFF.

LUCKY FOR YOU THEY DID. YOU'D PROBABLY BE DEAD BY NOW IF THEY HADN'T.

SATISFIED WITH TED'S EXPLANATION, THE MEN RETURNED TO THEIR STATIONS.

THE JAPS HAD MOVED ON AND THE SUB HAD MOVED ON, BUT PETER WAS STILL LEFT WITH THE PROBLEM OF WHAT TO DO ABOUT ANGELFISH.

THE JAPS ARE BOUND TO FIND HER SOONER OR LATER. WE CAN'T JUST LEAVE IT. WE'LL HAVE TO DESTROY HER. BUT I'M TEMPTED . . .

. . . TO PUT THE AMERICAN CREW BACK ON BOARD, SIR? IT WOULD CERTAINLY HELP MATTERS IF THEY COULD GET HER GOING AGAIN.

A PLAN WAS HATCHING IN DICK'S MIND. HE HURRIED AWAY TO FIND TED AND GET HIS OPINION.

WHEN HE HEARD WHAT WAS PLANNED, TED OFFERED TO HELP IN ANY WAY POSSIBLE.

WE CAN GIVE YOU A HAND WITH THE DEPTH-CHARGE, AND WE'VE GOT PLENTY AIR CYLINDERS AND MASKS. IT'S WORTH A TRY.

YEAH! AND THE DAMAGE TO THE BATTERIES CAN'T BE TOO BAD. I CHECKED THEM MYSELF JUST BEFORE THE CREW WENT ASHORE.

SO IT WAS SETTLED. THE TWO CREWS WOULD WORK TOGETHER TO REFLOAT ANGELFISH.

BUT THE PROBLEM OF THE CROCS STILL REMAINED AS THE BRITISH SUBMARINE SURFACED IN THE INLET UNDER COVER OF DARKNESS, AFTER A CAUTIOUS APPROACH.

ALL SET TO GO, SIR. I'M TAKING JUST A FEW MEN DOWN TO HELP SORT THINGS OUT. TED'S COMING TOO.

RIGHT. WE'LL STAND BY WITH THE MACHINE GUNS.

ONLY DICK HAD TO SUIT-UP, THEN THE PARTY OF DIVERS COULD LEAVE FOR ANGELFISH.

AFTER PADDLING CAUTIOUSLY TO WHERE THE SUBMARINE LAY, THEY PREPARED TO DIVE—BUT TED INSISTED ON GOING FIRST.

IT'S MY BOAT, AND IF THE CROCS WANT A MEAL THEN I GUESS THAT'S MY RESPONSIBILITY TOO.

DICK COULDN'T ARGUE WITH THAT. THE AMERICAN WAS DETERMINED TO HELP.

HURRIEDLY THEY MADE THEIR WAY DOWN, AND SLIPPED ONE BY ONE INTO THE CONNING TOWER.

SAFELY INSIDE, THE FIRST TASK WAS TO REFLOAT THE SUB.

NOTHING MUCH I CAN DO TO HELP. THEY SEEM TO KNOW WHAT THEY'RE DOING ANYWAY.

THE OPERATION WENT AHEAD WITHOUT ANY HITCHES AS THE AMERICANS ADJUSTED THE CONTROLS.

DUE TO THE SKILL OF THE BOMB DISPOSAL TEAM, THEIR TASK WAS SOON COMPLETED.

THAT'S IT MATES.

AS THE BOMB ROLLED OVERBOARD, DICK AND TED CAME BACK OUT ON TO THE BRIDGE.

OVER SHE GOES!

GOOD! WE CAN TRANSFER THE REST OF YOUR CREW NOW.

BUT SUDDENLY TED'S ATTENTION WAS DRAWN TO A BRIEF FLICKER OF LIGHT ON THE SHORE.

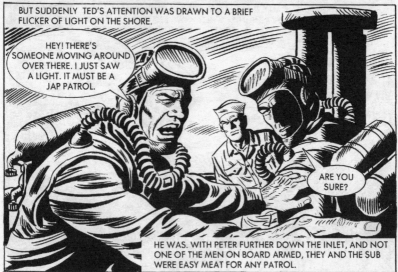

HEY! THERE'S SOMEONE MOVING AROUND OVER THERE. I JUST SAW A LIGHT. IT MUST BE A JAP PATROL.

ARE YOU SURE?

HE WAS. WITH PETER FURTHER DOWN THE INLET, AND NOT ONE OF THE MEN ON BOARD ARMED, THEY AND THE SUB WERE EASY MEAT FOR ANY PATROL.

SWIFTLY TED'S CREW TRANSFERRED BACK TO THEIR OWN VESSEL. AMIDST ALL THE PREPARATIONS, PETER MADE A FINAL EFFORT TO PERSUADE THE AMERICAN TO LEAVE IMMEDIATELY, ALTHOUGH IT WAS LOW TIDE.

WE'LL HAVE TO SURFACE FOR THIS SECTION, AND IF YOU'RE NOT QUICK YOU'LL HAVE TO DO IT IN BROAD DAYLIGHT.

WE'LL BE RIGHT BEHIND YOU. ALL WE'VE TO DO IS SEE TO THE BATTERIES, THEN WE'RE OFF.

SATISFIED WITH THIS, PETER RETURNED TO HIS SUB, TAKING DICK WITH HIM.

MINUTES LATER, TAMARIN MOVED OUT TO SEA LEAVING THE AMERICANS BEHIND — WITH A PROBLEM.

WE'VE ONLY HALF POWER, BUT WE'LL STILL NEED AN HOUR.

MAKE THAT HALF-AN-HOUR — UNLESS YOU WANT THE JAPS TREADING ON YOUR TAIL!

THE DEPARTURE OF THE BRITISH WAS A LOT MORE OBVIOUS THAN THEIR ARRIVAL.

AM I GLAD TO BE AWAY FROM THERE!

WE'LL BE CLEAR OF THE REEFS IN FIVE MINUTES, SIR.

THEN, WITH BARELY ENOUGH ROOM TO SUBMERGE, THEIR LUCK RAN OUT AS A PATROLLING JAP SEAPLANE PILOT SAW THEIR WAKE AGAINST THE DARK SEA.

ALREADY THE ENEMY KITE WAS BORING IN TO ATTACK.

AS ITS BOMBS HURTLED MERCILESSLY TOWARDS THE TARGET, PLUNGING DEEP INTO THE BLACK WATER, THE JAP NAVIGATOR RADIOED SOME NEARBY NAVAL UNITS TO COME AND TAKE UP THE CHASE.

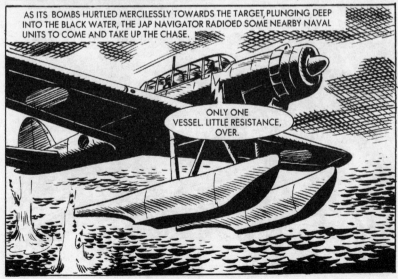

TAMARIN HAD APPARENTLY ESCAPED UNDAMAGED, BUT THE AIRCRAFT REMAINED CIRCLING OVERHEAD UNTIL THE JAP WARSHIPS ARRIVED.

A FRIGATE AND A COUPLE OF SMALLER SUBMARINE-CHASERS HEADING THIS WAY. WE'LL GO DEEP AND TRY TO DODGE THEM.

AYE, AYE, SIR.

UNKNOWN TO PETER, THE BOMBS HAD CAUSED A FUEL TANK TO LEAK, LEAVING A TRAIL OF OIL FOR THE ENEMY TO FOLLOW, SHOWING EVERY TWIST OF THEIR COURSE.

SO, THE SUBMARINE HAS TURNED AWAY AGAIN. MAKE ANOTHER RUN ON ONE-TWENTY DEGREES.

WITH THE SEAPLANE NOW ACTING AS SPOTTER FOR THE ENEMY SHIPS BELOW, THEIR DEPTH-CHARGING BECAME INCREASINGLY ACCURATE.

WITH ALL THE POWER SHE COULD MUSTER, SHE PLOUGHED THROUGH THE MIST AT HIGH SPEED TOWARDS THE VAGUE SILHOUETTE OF AN ENEMY VESSEL.

SHIP AHEAD, SIR.

IT'S A JAP FRIGATE. STAND BY TO FIRE TORPEDOES!

THE JAPANESE WERE TOO PREOCCUPIED WITH TAMARIN TO NOTICE THIS NEW DANGER . . .

. . . UNTIL A TORPEDO RIPPED A GAPING HOLE IN THE FRIGATE'S HULL.

AAAIIIEEE!

THIS VESSEL WAS NOW OUT OF THE FIGHT.

HOWEVER, TED SOON HAD ANOTHER PROBLEM ON HIS MIND.

DRAT! THE MIST'S CLEARING. OUR RADAR WON'T BE AS USEFUL IN GOOD VISIBILITY.

THAT WAS THE END OF THEIR SNEAK ATTACKS.

NOW THE ODDS FAVOURED THE REMAINING FASTER, MORE MANOEUVRABLE JAP SHIPS — ESPECIALLY WHEN THE AMERICANS' RADAR PACKED UP SCANT SECONDS AFTER THEY ENGAGED ONE OF THE VESSELS.

SHINTO! ANOTHER SUBMARINE. FIRE!

OF ALL THE TIMES OUR RADAR PICKS TO GO WRONG . . . AND WATCH YOUR SHOOTING! THAT ONE WENT WIDE.

BUT AGAIN THEIR LUCK CHANGED.

AAAIIEEE!

THEY SCORED A DIRECT HIT ON THE BRIDGE, WRECKING IT AND DAMAGING THE SHIP'S INSTRUMENTS.

THE AMERICANS WERE STILL IN TROUBLE. THEIR BIG GUN HAD JAMMED AND THE ENEMY WERE GETTING UNCOMFORTABLY ACCURATE — UNTIL SUDDENLY THE JAP CRAFT BLEW UP.

WHAT THE HECK WAS THAT? WE DIDN'T EVEN FIRE!

I THINK OUR LIMEY FRIENDS HAVE JOINED IN, SIR. THAT WAS A TORPEDO.

UNDER COVER OF THE SEA MIST, TAMARIN SURFACED, USING HER RADAR TO LOCATE THE REMAINING ENEMY SHIP WHOSE POSITION WAS SWIFTLY PASSED ON TO THE AMERICANS.

WHERE IS THIS SHOOTING COMING FROM? WE ARE SINKING!

BOTH SUBMARINES CONCENTRATED THEIR FIRE ON THE INVISIBLE TARGET, PUTTING AN END TO IT — AND THE CONFLICT.

THERE WAS NO TIME TO CELEBRATE AS HOSTILE AIRCRAFT WOULD BE APPROACHING, ALERTED BY THE BEATEN JAPS.

THANKS FOR YOUR HELP. SEE YOU IN AUSTRALIA?

SURE THING, PAL. WE'LL BE WAITING.

THE SUBMARINES SLID SILENTLY BENEATH THE WAVES, BOTH CREWS IN GOOD SPIRITS.

I WONDER WHO'S GOING TO GET BACK FIRST. THE YANKS OR US?

PROBABLY US. YOU KNOW HOW ACCIDENT PRONE TED'S TUB IS!

BUT TED HAD FORGOTTEN THE STATE OF HIS BATTERIES, SO WHEN HE REACHED PORT, TAMARIN WAS WAITING.

RADIO MESSAGE FROM THE LIMEYS, SIR. THEY SAY THEY WERE JUST ABOUT TO COME AND FIND US.

I GUESS THEY'VE EARNED THEIR JOKE. ASK 'EM IF THEY'VE GOT ANY DRINKS LINED UP FOR US.

AS SOON AS THE AMERICANS DOCKED THEY HURRIED ASHORE TO CELEBRATE. THE NAVAL POLICE WAITED FOR THE FIRST BRAWL TO BREAK OUT, BUT THEY WEREN'T NEEDED . . .

. . . FOR IN THE SAVAGE FIGHTING, THE CREW OF ANGELFISH HAD LEARNED THAT THEY COULD NOT SURVIVE ALONE. WITH TED AS THEIR SKIPPER THEY FOUGHT ALONGSIDE THE ROYAL NAVY THROUGHOUT THE REST OF THE WAR, ROUTING THE ENEMY AND FREEING THE ISLANDS FROM THE TYRANNICAL GRASP OF THE JAPANESE.

Commando
**THE END**

# THE COVERS

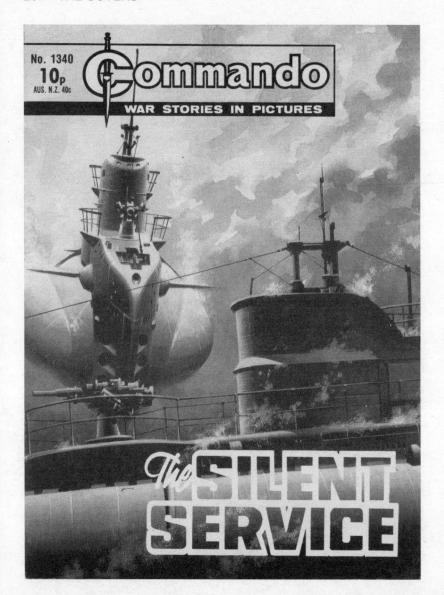